THE SIREN'S SONG

DEMONS AMONG US

THE SIREN'S SONG

KATELYN BREHM

Beneath the sea another world exists
It's tugging me by the ankles and my wrists
The morning wind come and pull me away
Out to where the dolphins play

— The Samples, "Feel Us Shaking"

CHAPTER ONE
ELIAS

OFF THE COAST OF SOUTH CAROLINA

Salt water glided across my skin like silk, its cool bite the ideal temperature for a long swim. The April sun newly escaped from its winter purgatory shone bright, adding a touch of warmth to the Atlantic and creating perfection. The hours I spent in the water slipped by, the movement of my body synchronized to the swell of the ocean.

Complete freedom. Life didn't get much better.

Rhythmic splashing announced another swimmer closing fast. I slowed my pace and treaded water to allow him to catch up. Within moments, my cousin and best friend popped his head out of the waves. He flipped his dark hair out of his face and swam along next to me.

"Sorry I'm late." Niko's breath labored with exertion.

"Rough night last night?"

He lifted a shoulder out of the water and tilted his head to meet it. A total non-answer.

"You went home with someone again last night, didn't you?" I taunted.

He glowered at me over a tight mouth.

Amusement stretched my smirk into a smile. This was going to be fun. "Let me guess…" I cleared my throat, ready to mock him for the millionth time about his hopeless romanticism. "You met an incredible woman. You had this instant connection you just had to explore."

He looked away with a huff and squinted at the horizon.

Bingo.

"This is starting to become a habit, Niko. A bad habit."

He turned back to throw daggers at me with his eyes, and I laughed at his ridiculous indignation. "You're so predictable."

"What do you want, E? I was having a great time. She's a scientist and got to tellin' me about her research. I was hungry, so—"

"So, you asked her to dinner and ended up talking all night." The number of times I'd heard that same story… "You can't keep doing this every time you sing."

"Why not? What's wrong with gettin' to know someone?"

"Seriously?" I shook my head and blinked in disbelief. He couldn't possibly be that thick-skulled.

"Expectations, Niko. Expectations and drama." I'd learned that lesson in my twenties—I was all set with clingy, territorial women trying to change my routine. "You ready for a relationship with this woman? You think she'll let you spend four hours a day swimming? Late nights singing to audiences full of women with the same objective she had when she went out to dinner with you?" I cocked an eyebrow.

"You're a cynic."

"I'm a realist."

He scoffed.

"She's not going to be happy when you don't call her." The words came out automatic and chiding, not the first time I'd voiced that particular warning.

As sirens, the last thing we needed was outright rejection, but a nonexistent audience came in a close second. Our song demanded an answer, and we were physically compelled to fill the adoration well or pay the price.

"Not sure how you plan on satisfying your compulsion in front of an audience full of scorned lovers," I said.

Niko narrowed his eyes. "Maybe I *will* call her," he clapped back, challenge thick in his voice.

I snorted. "No, you won't. If you called every woman you sang to and then took out to dinner, we'd never swim again—you'd be too busy on the phone."

He twisted his face into a sneer and shoved his hand into the water, sending a splash over my head.

I chuckled and flipped the hair out of my face. At

least when I sang to someone, I kept them at arm's length—a few drinks, a little dancing, a *lot* of flirting. And if I was lucky? If the situation was right? Some no-strings-attached casual sex. But that was it. No dinner. No expectations. No regrets.

"Trying to find something more meaningful than a one-night stand isn't gonna kill you, E. I swear, you have the emotional depth of a puddle."

I gasped and smacked the back of my hand to my forehead. "You wound me."

He rolled his eyes.

"Golf tournament's this weekend," he said after a beat. "Island's gonna be crawlin' with tourists."

"Shit! I forgot. Right on."

He nodded. "Shelter Cove's gonna be packed tonight for open mic."

"Hell yeah. I'm in."

My siren's compulsion stirred, imagining the audience, its thirst for attention a slow heat that crept through my insides urging me to unleash my voice. Our song created a deep and powerful pull, far stronger than our speaking voices, and I was all about big impact.

"Let's get going," I said, impatient to move. "I want to get a couple more hours in before we head back. I get cranky when I'm not in the water long enough."

"You and me both, cuz."

"I'll race you to that shoal we found last week. Loser gets the winner's front desk duty for a week."

Niko didn't stand a chance. I had a full night's

sleep and motivation—I despised desk shifts. Anything that took me away from the water was torture.

He flashed his wide, toothy grin, face bright with an excitement that matched my own. "You're on."

I plunged beneath the surface, dolphin-kicked as far as my breath could take me, and settled into my stroke. Flying through the ocean in harmony with the waves, my soul echoed the sights and sounds of its watery home.

Why would anyone risk this for a relationship? What could one woman give me that the ocean and the allure of my voice didn't already provide? Especially when the odds of finding a woman who'd accept my nature and respect my need for independence were... not in my favor. A creature like that was more mythical than a siren.

CHAPTER TWO
LENA

SEA PINES, HILTON HEAD ISLAND,
SOUTH CAROLINA

The key to Grandma's house was under the doormat right where the lawyer said it would be. I flipped it over in my hand wondering how things would be without her. Would the house still look like home? Smell like home? Feel like home? Only one way to find out.

I willed my arm to move and wiggled the key into the lock. I turned the knob of the forest-green door, mossy with age and the incessant humidity, and shoved it open with a bump of my hip. I'd nagged her for years to fix the old door. The task fell to me, now.

Stepping across the threshold into the hallway of my past, I held on to the doorknob like an anchor to the present. The rising tension in my chest threatened to strangle me, but I refused to start crying. I inhaled deeply, held my breath to recenter, and exhaled long and slow. One sob session per day; that's all I'd allowed myself since Grandma died.

I tossed the key onto the entry table. It struck the glass with a clatter and created a trail through the thin coat of dust—dust that wouldn't have been there a week ago. She'd always kept the house pristine.

The house's musty scent—salt air infused with damp moss, the soft, comforting fragrance of the Lowcountry, of my childhood home—suffused my senses. But something new punctuated the familiar smell. Emptiness. It had only been a week since my grandma passed and the house had been locked up, but staleness changed the quality of the air. It sucked the life right out of it and reminded me of what I'd lost.

I padded across the living room's plush carpet into the kitchen. This is where I'd always remember her. Sitting at the kitchen table balancing the ledger of her herbalism shop. Eating her lunch watching deer graze outside the bay window. Hovering over the standing mixer whipping cream to top the coconut cake she made for my birthday. The kitchen was the center of the house and our family of two. The ghost of our lives —the ghost of her life—lingered there, and I held on to it with desperation, not wanting to admit I was alone.

The woman who'd raised me, the only family I'd ever known, was gone. I'd never see her again. Never curl up on the couch with her and watch TV. Never eat cinnamon toast with her at midnight. Never feel her arms wrap around me in unconditional love.

The hole Grandma's absence left in my heart ached with each breath. I braced myself on the edge of the island and let my head drop trying to breathe through the abyss of my loneliness.

"Come on, Lena," I mumbled in a feeble attempt at self-encouragement. "You know how to breathe. You teach your students how to breathe for Chrissake. Pull it together."

I'm not sure how long I stood there breathing through the persistent lump that had plagued my throat since I'd received the news of her passing. But eventually my legs stopped shaking and the lump shrunk enough my breath no longer shuddered.

My nerves back under some semblance of control, I needed to get on with my day. Responsibility called. I wandered into the living room and curled up cross-legged on my corner of the couch. I pulled out my phone and brought up the number for my studio in Charleston.

"Yoga Star Charleston. This is Candace. How can I help you?"

"Hey, Candy. It's Lena."

"Lena! How are you?" Her usually peppy voice dripped with sympathy, swelling the lump in my throat. This would be much easier if she just pretended my life wasn't falling apart.

"I'm fine. I promised I'd call when I got in so... I'm here. How are things at the studio?"

The studio didn't really worry me; it practically ran itself these days. Candace was a fantastic office manager, not to mention instructor, and this wasn't the first time I'd left the studio in her capable hands while I visited the island.

"Same. Busy. We always get that little bump during Easter break."

"Every year."

An awkward silence fell over the line filled with our mutual disdain for the next inevitable topic. I inhaled deeply, puffed out my cheeks, and blew the air out long and slow through pursed lips.

"Did he drop it off?"

"Yup." Venom filled Candy's clipped reply. She didn't like him any more than I did.

Okay, not true. I liked him less.

"It's over then," I whispered, the words a mere shadow of my wonder and relief.

"It is. I checked the papers myself to make sure he signed everything correctly—I don't trust that man, Lena—but they're all in order. I put them in the safe."

And just like that, my marriage was over. I'd filed for divorce months ago, but it had never felt final. Not until now. Those papers released his half of the studio back to me, the last vestige of a string of bad decisions excised from my life. The final tie was broken. Broken like his promises. Broken like my faith in men. Broken like my heart.

A million tiny paper cuts of conflicting emotions attacked my insides, slicing at different angles to destroy the remnants of my shattered spirit. The lump returned, choking me, this time a combination of relief, failure, and frustration.

I massaged my throat and released a shuddering breath. "Thanks, Candy. I'm... I'm glad it's finally over." I fidgeted with the fringe of the couch throw to distract myself from the harsh realities of the conversation. It didn't work. "I never have to see him again." I should have been overjoyed, but the words came out resigned and defeated.

"This is a good thing, Lena. You know this. That relationship turned toxic years ago. He strung you along, not letting go of the studio. And for what? Just to mess with you, if you ask me. Asshole."

I huffed. Candy never swore, but made an exception when talking about my ex.

And he really was an asshole. A lying, cheating, manipulative asshole.

"It's just... It's just a lot right now. All at once."

"I know. It is. But a wise yoga instructor once told me, 'the only way out is through.'"

I snorted at my former student throwing my words back at me. "I didn't make that up, you know."

"It's no less true."

"You're not wrong." I paused. As difficult as it was for me to take a step back, I had no choice. "Look, Candy, I don't know how long I'm going to be down here. There's so much to sort out with the house..."

"Don't worry. Take all the time you need. The schedule is staffed for the next three months with subs available. I've got the business side of things covered, and new instructor training doesn't start for two months. There's no rush to get back."

A fresh sting flared in my chest, her words lemon juice squeezed over all those paper cuts. Apart from the studio, Candy, and a handful of devoted students, there wasn't anything left for me in Charleston. My marriage was over. We'd sold the house in the divorce. He'd won most of our friends. And if my own studio didn't need me...

I knew that wasn't what Candy meant. She was trying to give me space, be supportive, but her words landed hard for all the simple truth they contained.

"No, you're right; there's no rush. Call me if you need anything, and I'll let you know my plans in a couple days. If I come up with a plan."

"Whenever you're ready. I'm here for ya, babe."

"Thanks, Candy," I said, relieved that the peppiness had returned to her voice. I needed some normal.

"I got you, Lena. Take care."

I set my phone down on the coffee table and sank into the couch, unsure what to do with myself next. The house felt hollow in my grandma's absence, a discarded shell washed up on shore, empty and forgotten. Thoughts of the past churned and clashed with worries about the future. They fused to form a heaviness that weighed on my shoulders and settled onto my chest.

I was spiraling. I needed to return to the present, an impossible feat sitting in that house surrounded by the past. Time for a change of scenery. I wrenched myself off the couch and marched out the front door, determined to regain purchase over my runaway mind.

The winding path to the beach snaked through live oaks dripping with Spanish moss, and loblolly pines speared the sky with questing branches. Through the thick canopy, sunlight dappled the sandy walkway. Cicadas chirruped their persistent song, and pine needles crunched underfoot releasing their fragrant scent. It combined with magnolia and ocean salt to suffuse the warm, humid air with a sweet perfume unique to Hilton Head.

Grandma said magic lived on the island, and as I wound my way through the old trees, the other-worldly energy flooded my senses, making it feel as though I walked through a dream.

I emerged from the dense tree cover to a wooden bridge crossing one of the waterways that connected the swampy lagoons of Sea Pines. A turtle poked its head out of the water, and I stopped to scan the banks for alligators. That late in the afternoon, the sun had begun its slow descent, and without its mid-day heat, the gators retreated to their swampy homes. Maybe tomorrow.

Across the bridge, the path grew sandier, and the smell of saltwater pierced my nostrils. My pace quick-ened with anticipation, and soon, I crested the dune, and the clear blue expanse of the Atlantic materialized before me.

If the sights, sounds, and smells of the island weren't enough to prove the presence of magic, emerging from the tree cover onto a white beach kissed by cerulean waves would make anyone a believer.

I kicked off my sandals and sank my feet into the warm sand, squishing the soft grit between my toes with each step. At the water's edge, the cool surf lapped my ankles, and the ocean breeze caressed my face. The crash of the waves and the distant cry of gulls provided the scene's soothing melody.

I closed my eyes and tilted my face up to the sun, longing to feel something—anything—besides loss. And for a moment, I was truly present. I forgot about my grandma, the house, my failed marriage, the fear of being so completely alone, and was present to the controlled cadence of my breath, rising and falling in time with the rhythmic surge of the ocean.

Splashing broke the spell of my meditative escape, and I opened my eyes. Two sets of arms cut through the surf, powerful swimmers coming up from the south.

Annoyed by the interruption, I waded deeper into the water and shut my eyes, desperate to regain my peace. The swimmers moved through the water with efficiency and grace, the churn of their strokes fluid and regular. I added their music to the harmony of the waves and my breath.

The hypnotizing beat slowed, and I reopened my eyes to find two men emerging from the break. They stood, and my body sparked like a live wire. Two perfect specimens of male physique shook water from their hair and waded through the waist-deep water. They had to be professional swimmers—tall and lean, with broad, muscled shoulders and washboard abs. *Oh, gods above...* The water dipped below their knees revealing thick quads beneath tight swim shorts. *Damn.* Bodies like those in trunks like those should be illegal.

I blinked hard to regain focus. My lusty body staged a coup of my brain any time I encountered a well-built, athletic body. Not good. I beat down the revolution by reminding myself that my affinity for muscles is what had landed me with my ex-husband. Turns out a nice body doesn't necessarily translate into a nice guy. Who'd have thought.

I swiveled my gaze away from the eye candy and focused on the horizon. Meditation. Breathing. Right.

CHAPTER THREE
ELIAS

I shook the water from my hair and trudged through the knee-deep break toward the beach, invigorated from the exercise and eager for the night's performance. "Good swim. Feeling more awake?"

"You know it." Niko stretched his arms behind his back.

"Nice." I clapped him on the shoulder. "All set for a night out and a week of front desk duty."

He groaned and slumped his shoulders.

"And remember—no need to turn tonight into a first date. Just take the adoration hit and move on." He rolled his eyes and shrugged off my hand.

"I'm serious, man. It's in our nature. Embrace it."

Niko's forehead creased and jaw worked as if chewing on an idea. "Don't you ever want something more? Something deeper?"

"No." Simple. Definitive. True. "I don't."

He stared at me blankly for a moment before shaking his head. But who in their right mind would tether themselves to a single person when an entire ocean of possibilities lay before them? Not me. The rush of flexing my song's power and basking in adoration slaked any thirst I had for connection. All without strings. I didn't need anything more, and someday, Niko would realize that's all he needed as a siren.

"Good thing your dad didn't feel that way, or you wouldn't be here."

I stopped, chuffed out a snort, and held up my hand to count on each finger the reasons he was full of shit. "One: Dad got Mom pregnant. Two: he wasn't an asshole, so he proposed even though he'd only known her for all of two months. Which, three: absolutely changed his life. And four: he was lucky Mom didn't freak when she found out he was a siren and that she was pregnant with a demon baby."

"Okay, okay." Niko held up both palms, relenting. "But you forgot five: regardless of how they got there, your parents, and my parents, love the hell out of each other and wouldn't change things for the world. I'm just saying, E, something more is possible."

I shook my head. Maybe, but he'd never convince me that possible was worth the drama of finding it or the risk of rejection. I was perfectly content being a bachelor.

We emerged from the water, and my attention snapped to a flash of pale blonde in my periphery. A woman stood knee-deep among the shallow waves, eyes closed, face lifted to the wind. Her hair, so pale it was almost white, was tied high on her head, the long ponytail a waterfall of sunshine cascading past her neck and ending between sculpted shoulders. Wisps of hair floated around her freckled face in a halo of morning light.

My eyes travelled the length of her magnificent body. She wore cropped yoga pants that hugged powerful yet slender legs, and she had an ass that made my hands fist. She held her hips, and her shapely, muscled arms, tinted pink from the sun, stood out against her flowy tank top. She had to be an athlete. What a beauty.

I licked my lips and, with my gaze still laser-beam focused on my newly acquired target, tapped Niko on the shoulder. "Gimme a minute."

He stepped alongside me. "Seriously, E? You can't wait till we go out tonight?"

"And pass up an opportunity like that? Are you kidding?"

"She looks like she wants to be alone."

I tore my eyes away from her killer curves and considered Niko. He watched the woman, his head tilted and mouth shaped into a frown.

I followed his gaze, trying to see what had him making that face, but my eyes landed on her ass in those yoga pants, and desire replaced any ability for rational thought.

"Maybe," I admitted. "But not for long."

I toweled off, ran a hand through my hair to tame

its post-swim disarray, and strode over to my target. My power surfaced as I closed in, my instincts urging me to entice her with my voice.

"Hi." I wove my siren's call into that single syllable.

She blinked her eyes open and turned to face me, full lips parted in surprise. Or was that irritation? It didn't matter.

"Hello." Her voice was quiet, but rich and husky. She scanned my face for the briefest moment, then fixed her eyes back on the water.

What the hell?

"I'm Elias Georgiou." I introduced myself slowly, drawing out the words and threading them with invitation. "I don't recognize you. Are you here for the tournament?"

"No."

Her eyes never left the horizon. Why wasn't she batting her lashes? Reaching out to touch my arm? Where was her smile? Her attention?

Determined, I thickened the power in my voice. "Just visiting then?"

She faced me with narrowed eyes as if studying an unwelcome blemish. "You seem determined to have a conversation. All right. Here it is." She folded her Linda-Hamilton-in-Terminator-Two arms across her chest and held me in place with an equally fierce stare. "My grandma—my only family—passed away last week, and I'm here to deal with her estate. I just came from her—now my—empty house after a real upbeat phone call about finalizing my divorce. So, yeah, not really in the mood for small talk."

Her harsh tone lashed me like a whip, and I winced. "Sorry. I didn't mean to intrude. You were alone, and I thought you might enjoy some company."

She glared at the water, nostrils flaring with quickened breath, and tapped an impatient finger on her arm.

She wanted me gone, but an unrelenting force pushed me to try again. Maybe it was my siren's compulsion. Or maybe it was the challenge of her indifference. Or maybe it was her lower lip sticking out in a sexy pout begging to be kissed...

I blinked hard to clear my head of that mental image. Whatever the case, I craved her attention.

"Look." I opened my arms in an inviting gesture. "If you want to take your mind off things for a while, there's an open mic tonight at Shelter Cove. Sometimes the best medicine is a change of scenery." I flung a thumb over my shoulder. "Niko and I will be there." I shrugged, trying to affect casual indifference even though my stomach roiled at the possibility of rejection. "Might help to relax with some drinks and music."

"Thanks. I'll think about it." She unfolded her arms and showed me her back.

A quick breath escaped me, her perfunctory words a verbal elbow to my gut. I hesitated, dumbfounded by her lack of interest and nauseated from her denial. But...

She hadn't said no. And I'd only used my speaking voice. A full-on rejection of my song would have left me in far worse condition. For all the strength and satisfaction I gained from my siren's compulsion, the flip side of the deal was not great. I had to take her open-ended rebuff as a win. "Hope to see you there."

The generic words died on the wind, and stunned by her blatant disinterest, I walked away.

I ignored the smug expression on Niko's face, grabbed my towel, and started hightailing it back to our beach house. He fell in step beside me, shaking his head in a way that let me know he thought I was an idiot.

"You're so single-minded. You didn't even bother to read her, did you?"

My head snapped up in confusion, and Niko's smug expression transformed into a judgmental frown. "You're unbelievable. You didn't feel that? How much pain she was in? I felt it, and I wasn't even talking to her!"

Sirens had emotional intuition, a type of empathy that went far beyond instinct. It allowed us to experience other's attraction, adoration, and devotion, to soak up those emotions and satisfy our siren's compulsion. Unfortunately, the ability wasn't limited to those feelings.

"Really?" I grimaced, a twinge of guilt adding to my discomfort, and glanced over my shoulder to where the woman stood hugging herself and gazing out over the ocean. "No, I suppose I didn't."

"Grief, fear, loneliness—they were rolling off her in waves. It's no wonder she blew you off. Your speaking voice alone would've been hard-pressed to cut through all that." Niko regarded me with serious intent, eyes steady and assessing, mouth stern. We'd known each other our entire lives, and he'd never looked at me with such judgment. "And I don't believe you'd be heartless enough to try."

"No." I shoved a hand into my hair and tugged hard at the strands. "No, I'd never do that. I should have read her."

He clapped me on the shoulder and gave it a squeeze. "Just making sure."

Something inside me dislodged at the thought of that sharp-tongued, sexy goddess in pain. It banged on my chest for attention like a crazed beast rattling the bars of a cage.

I craved her undivided attention, the compulsion to sing to her and secure her adoration unrelenting. But Niko was right; I wasn't a monster. And this reaction—this thing inside my chest—it didn't feel like my siren's instinct. I wanted to talk to her, soothe her, brush my thumb across those pouty lips.

I shook out my arms, rocked my head from side to side, and rolled my shoulders, trying to dispel those unwelcome thoughts and the nausea that still lingered from her earlier rejection. But despite my efforts to forget the chance encounter and focus on the upcoming night, a seed of hope sprouted that I might see her again and get another chance.

CHAPTER FOUR
LENA

I walked through the front door of the house only to change my clothes and walk back out less than ten minutes later. I hopped on my beach cruiser and pedaled north toward Coligny Square along the canopied bike paths that traversed the forests and golf courses dominating the southern half of the island. Coligny was on the opposite end of Sea Pines from my grandma's house, but the shopping center hosted the only hot yoga studio on the island. I told myself the forty-minute ride was worth it, that I needed to step onto my mat. But as the heat of the practice room permeated my body and I moved through my flow, pretense departed as quickly as sweat. Stripped bare, I stood at the top of my space left only with the truth—I was avoiding the house and with it my future.

I progressed through my vinyasa, flowing from one pose to the next while acknowledging my current state of mind—I didn't want to make any decisions. Decisions meant committing to a path that moved past my failed marriage, past my grandma's death, and into an uncertain future. Alone.

I had to choose a direction. I had to transition to the next pose. But staying stagnant and dwelling in the space between lives—between poses—seemed much easier than admitting I stood at a crossroads.

That's why I came to my mat. The challenges I faced in my practice mirrored the hard lessons and truths I needed to learn in life. So, I stood in my emotional discomfort just as I stood in my physical discomfort. I admitted I wasn't ready to move on, and for now, avoidance was the sum total of my plan. And that was okay.

And avoidance was also how I found myself standing at the entrance of Shelter Cove later that night.

After yoga, I'd fully intended on spending a peaceful night at home with my journal and a book, but the deafening silence of the empty house gnawed at my attention. I'd barely jotted down a few words before I snapped the journal shut and tossed it onto the coffee table. I needed to get out of that house and out of my head. I needed distraction. Something to lighten the mood.

I got in my car and headed out of Sea Pines toward the northern half of the island. As I drove, two swimmers emerging from the ocean in short, tight swim trunks flashed across my mind's eye, and the silken words of the man who'd approached me resounded in my thoughts. I blinked away the memory and turned up the radio, beating my thumb against the steering wheel in time to the music in a vain attempt to deafen the voice.

Going to Shelter Cove had absolutely nothing to do with those chiseled bodies from the beach. Nothing at all. I'd sworn off men with playboy personas, and the moment Elias had introduced himself to me, klaxons rang like I was on the bridge of the Enterprise. Red Alert!

I knew the type; I'd married one. Been there. Done that. Have the t-shirt and want to burn it in a trash fire. The asshole left with half our savings after I paid off all his student loans, bought him a car, and added him as joint owner of the yoga studio. *My* yoga studio. The yoga studio I built from nothing. Student by student. Class by class. None of which was as important to him as the twenty-something I'd found standing in our kitchen in her underwear after returning home early from a visit to the island.

Never again. Never again would I trust a smooth-talking, good-looking man. At least not with my heart.

King Neptune held his trident aloft, ready to smite the visitors milling about the bar and in front of the stage, bronze arms glinting under the lights strung between palmettos in front of the Shelter Cove marina. Music wafted through the damp night air, and the strange but familiar combination of magnolia and low tide filled my nostrils.

I scanned the crowd as I walked to the bar. Who was I kidding? I'd been drawn here tonight and not just by the need for distraction. There was something about Elias, something about his voice. He hadn't said much on the beach, but even now, the hypnotic quality of his words reverberated through my head, quietly shouting for my attention.

I brushed the hair out of my face and blinked hard, trying to jar his voice out of my brain. I came tonight to distract myself with music. No hot swimmers with sultry voices necessary.

The golf tournament usually coincided with Easter break—around mid-April—and brought all manner of tourists to the island. This year was no different, and Shelter Cove was packed. Sitting at the bar, I ordered a brandy and diet and tapped my foot to the young Joni Mitchell performing on stage. Kids chased after each other while others waited patiently in line to get their faces painted. Couples shared drinks. Families gathered around picnic tables. Men and women in their twenties gathered in groups laughing and drinking.

The scene put an exclamation point at the end of my life's sentence—You are alone!—each smiling couple, each doting parent, and each needy child a reminder of everything I didn't have. I clenched my teeth and tried to breathe through the heaviness resettling itself atop my shoulders.

Screw it. I grabbed my drink and gulped half of it down. Maybe this hadn't been the best idea.

The singer finished, and the few people paying

attention politely clapped. I spun on my stool to face the stage and nearly choked on my drink. There he was. The swimmer. Elias.

He sauntered onto the stage and up to the mic with an easy stride, carrying an acoustic guitar by its neck. He wore a white linen shirt over khaki shorts, sleeves casually pushed up to his elbows, the loose fabric unbuttoned enough to reveal the top of his strong, tanned chest. His angular face showcased a Hollywood smile—straight white teeth behind a crooked bend to a wide mouth. His hair had been wet when I'd seen him on the beach, but now sandy-blond, sun-bleached waves hung over his ears and forehead like he'd stepped off the set of a surfing movie.

Gods, he was gorgeous. How had I not noticed before?

Probably because you weren't a half brandy-and-diet deep.

Right.

He slung the guitar strap across his muscled body and sat down, propping up his Birkenstock-clad feet on the bottom rung of the stool, and rested the guitar on his knee. He adjusted the mic and scanned the crowd.

By chance or by fate, our eyes locked, and his toothy grin widened. He winked, and an unexpected thrill tingled my spine, making me both excited and uncomfortable.

He finished his survey of the audience and leaned

into the mic. "I'm Elias. Thanks for coming out." His silken voice danced across my skin like a sensual caress. "This one's called 'Feel Us Shaking' by The Samples."

He cleared his throat, shifted his weight, and began plucking the guitar strings with ease, sliding the familiar opening notes into the din that filled the warm spring night.

I inhaled sharply, my jaw dropping in surprised wonder as each word of the first phrase reached my hungry ears. His tenor floated over the guitar chords, the tone and timbre of his voice carrying a powerful yet ethereal quality that seemed intertwined with the island's magical atmosphere. I wanted to bathe in the lush notes. The soothing texture of the song harmonized with my soul, a balm for my broken spirit.

I wasn't the only one captivated by Elias. Heads turned, gazes fixed, laughter and conversations quieted, the audience held prisoner by the dulcet notes of the man's mesmerizing voice.

The scene evoked memories of the local legends my grandma used to tell me about when I was a child: mythical creatures inhabited Hilton Head, enchanting unsuspecting victims with their song. Of course, the old stories were just that—old stories—but as Elias continued to sing, I felt entranced, drawn to him by his music. I quickly finished my drink, unsettled by his magnetism and needing the brandy to steady my nerves.

I returned my focus to the stage, the melody

pulling on my attention until I yielded to its relentless demands. I swayed in time to the beat, and thoughts of the house and my uncertain future fled, replaced by Elias's voice.

He captured my eyes again, and the thrill of his attention broadened its wings across my chest. Maybe it was a trick of the light, or the fact I'd finished my drink, but his eyes shone such a bright blue they appeared to glow. And in that moment, our eyes connecting us across the distance, the world fell away, and he sang only to me.

Diamond waves through sunglass days go by
So beautiful to be here and alive
Though I've built sometimes so hard did I survive?
Feel us shaking

His mouth turned up at the corners as he held my eyes through the phrase. Then he blinked and broke our connection, releasing me. He dropped his head and continued to strum his guitar.

A bow-wave of emotion swept away the flutter in my chest, replacing it with a lump that traveled into my throat. I swallowed hard to keep it down. The intent in his eyes combined with his bright smile... The meaning behind the words he sang with his seductive voice... They cracked open my shielded, shattered heart. I hadn't felt anything other than disappointment and loss for so long, I'd lost sight of a simple truth: it was beautiful to be here and alive.

I closed my eyes, relaxed my shoulders, and with a clear head, opened my heart to the music. Within moments, the vise grip strangling my soul started to release. Contentment bordering on happiness rose like the swell of the ocean, and I smiled for the first time since my grandma died.

The song ended, and a palpable hush fell over the cove. The audience sat in motionless silence for a heartbeat, then erupted with applause, loud whoops, and whistling. Elias stood amid the outpouring of praise, his blue eyes sparkling under the string of lights, and joyful pride spread across his handsome features. He lifted his guitar in one hand, waved to the audience with the other, and descended the steps into a standing ovation.

A group of women in their twenties rushed the stage. I couldn't hear much above the wild applause, but from their squeals and flailing arms, I knew they were gushing. One woman lightly touched his shoulder, and another sidled up, consuming the space next to him. I snorted and rolled my eyes.

The urge to unabashedly gush was strong, but I had no doubt his playboy tendencies matched his rakish good looks and seductive voice. No need for me to join the party; he already had plenty of fangirls throwing themselves at him. I signaled the bartender for my check and tossed my credit card onto the bar.

While I waited, an uncanny pull tugged at my chest, urging me to go to him, talk to him, tell him he had a glorious voice, and beg him to sing to me again.

But I broke free of its clutches. The scars of my past reminded me he was the same make and model as my ex-husband and set me free.

Besides, forty-one-year-old women didn't fangirl.

I signed the receipt, and as I got up to leave, noticed a lightness in my step as if a few weights had been removed from the emotional barbell I'd been carrying across my shoulders. A sliver of hope shined through my darkness. If nothing else, Elias's song reminded me that as dire as things seemed, I was alive, and life held beautiful potential.

CHAPTER FIVE
ELIAS

I finished my song, and euphoria amplified satisfaction, the applause and adoration emanating from the crowd answering my call and fulfilling the demands of my compulsion. The energy invigorated my body with emotional fuel. What a rush.

I climbed down the steps eager to find the woman from the beach among the sea of men and women pressing toward the stage. On any other night, I'd entertain their attention and soak up their praise like a sponge, quenching my siren's thirst. But not tonight. Tonight, my preoccupied mind had other plans. I craned my head over the crowd even as I answered questions and shook hands. *There*. She tossed her credit card onto the bar.

Wait, what? She was... leaving? How? I sang to her. Right to *her*. I'd poured power into those words.

Frantic, I excused myself from the group of adoring

fans and wove my way through the gauntlet of atten-tion toward the bar. I broke through the crowd just as she rose from her stool and slung her purse across her shoulder.

I tried my best at nonchalance despite the urgency gripping my insides. I stepped up to the bar, leaned in, and threaded my voice with as much allure as I could manage without singing. "Leaving so soon?"

Startled, she jerked around, and her eyes went wide when they met mine. Her full, glossy lips formed an "Oh," and she shifted her weight as if unsure what to do next.

"Elias." Her voice cracked halfway through my name, and she cleared her throat.

"Are you leaving? I was hoping we could have a drink."

"I..." She glanced over her shoulder toward the parking lot, then back to me, her brow furrowed. She parted her lips to say something, and I knew from the conflict playing across her face she was about to make an excuse and leave, but then her mouth snapped shut, and her features relaxed. "Sure. Why not?"

"Right on."

Relief loosened my tight muscles. The last thing I needed was the physical backlash of an outright rejec-tion. I pulled out her stool for her and sat down on the one next to it. She avoided eye contact and instead tried to flag the bartender.

I rested my elbow on the bar. "You have me at a disadvantage."

She gave me a sidelong glance. "I do?" She resumed her quest for the bartender, extending an arm and waving her hand. She finally caught his attention, and he came to take our order.

"You do. I still don't know your name."

Her head snapped up, eyebrows jumping toward her hairline.

Finally, I had her attention.

She scrunched her nose, and a hint of pink colored her freckled cheeks. "I never did mention my name on the beach, did I?" Her tone was half remorseful, half embarrassed. "I'm sorry. I'm Lena. Lena Sommer."

"Nice to officially meet you, Lena Sommer." I winked.

"Really." She leaned in and winced apologetically. "I'm so sorry. I wasn't in the best of moods earlier. I'm still not to be honest, but that's no reason to be rude."

"You're fine. I was just teasing. And we're here now, aren't we? Sharing a drink?"

The bartender returned and set our drinks on the bar. I lifted my beer. "Consider this a do over."

Her shoulders relaxed, and the corner of her mouth kicked up. "Done."

Someone tapped me on the shoulder, and I twisted on my stool to find a curvy redhead with too much makeup and too little clothing standing behind me. I should have seen this coming.

"Excuse me," she said. "Are you going to sing again tonight?" Her voice was high and flirty, and her question sounded more like a plea.

Time to let her down gently, make sure she'd come back another night. "No, not tonight," I said and plastered my face with regret. "But I sing here regularly. So does Niko—my friend who performed earlier? Maybe you'll catch us another time."

"Ohhh." She drew out the sound in a long whine, crossed her arms, and pouted. "I'm here for the golf tournament. I'm leaving Sunday."

What a shame.

She lingered for an awkward moment like a fly caught in honey, stuck there by my voice. I turned back to Lena who bit her lip, trying not to laugh, and sipped my beer.

"Have a good night then," the woman squeaked and flounced off.

Lena's resolve broke, and she snickered deeply, the husky quality of her voice making even her mocking sexy. She lifted an eyebrow, and there was more than a little judgment in that look.

"What?"

"You have quite the fan club."

I shrugged. She wasn't wrong.

She made a point of craning her neck to look over my shoulder, so I followed her gaze. Several women cast furtive glances in our direction, whispering, gesturing, giggling. I turned back to Lena who, for the first time since I'd met her, smiled, her grey eyes sparkling with amusement. I didn't care how many other women gawped at me as long as she continued to look at me with that combination of delight and mischief.

"Does this happen often?"

I shrugged again, not knowing what to say, because, well, it did. "I like music. I like to sing. It makes me happy, and it makes other people happy."

"That's an understatement. You're an excellent singer. Is that what you do for a living? Are you a musician?"

"No. I do it because I love it. I teach the occasional guitar lesson for the local kids, but singing is just for me."

"I'm surprised. Your performance was so professional, so moving." Her eyes grew distant, and her body relaxed as if she was reliving my performance and it brought her peace.

So, I *had* affected her.

"Thank you," I said sincerely. "I like to think my singing brings others as much joy as it brings me."

She stared down at her drink and ran a fingertip around the rim of the glass. "I haven't heard that song in years."

"It's a good song."

"It is."

"And it seemed like a good fit for tonight."

She tilted her head, and her eyes held mine in a pensive stare. "It was for me."

I nodded and swigged my beer. "Live music is special and, in my experience, even more special when it holds a message you need to hear."

"Hm." Her eyes returned to her drink, and the curve of her mouth turned down. She took a sip, winced, and tipped her glass in my direction. "You're perceptive."

"It wasn't that hard to see." I spun my beer bottle in one hand. "You have beautiful eyes, Lena, but there's sadness in them."

A flush warmed her cheeks, and she nervously tucked loose hairs behind her ear. "That obvious, huh?"

I chuckled. "Yeah. You looked like you needed a reminder of lightness and fun, the good things in life."

This was getting heavy, and I wasn't Niko. I didn't get into deep conversations with women I didn't know. And yet… "Wanna talk about it?"

What the hell? My brain hitched on the words escaping my mouth.

"With a complete stranger?" She gave me a wry look. "Not particularly."

She needed to talk to someone, that much was obvious, and I didn't need to be a siren to see it. Yes, I sensed the heaviness she emanated, but she wore her emotions in her expression and body language as obviously as the kids running around with their faces painted. Niko had been right. It was no wonder the full strength of my call had so little impact. The emotional burden she carried was heavy.

"Sometimes it's easier with a complete stranger," I said, nudging her along. "No history. No fear of judgment. Besides, I'm not a *complete* stranger. We met this afternoon. And now we both know each other's names."

"Not going to let me forget that, are you?"

"Nope."

"Fair enough."

She sighed, set her glass on the bar, and poked at the ice cubes with the stirrer. "My grandma passed away last week." Her delicate throat moved through a swallow, and my chest clenched at the wave of grief that washed over her as she said the words. "That's why I'm here. She and I... We used to live here together before I graduated high school. I've lived in Charleston since then but visited often. Maybe not as much in recent years."

Regret and bitterness laced those last words. She'd mentioned a divorce...

She rolled her shoulders as if she could shake off the new, toxic emotion.

"We were each other's only family. When she passed, I inherited everything. I'm trying to sort through it all. There's just so much"—she waved her hand in circles—"paperwork and the lawyer and the house and the gaping hole in my life and..."

Her voice wavered, and she stopped, her throat bobbing. She looked up from her drink with glassy eyes. "So, yeah. I'm trying to figure out what to do with all that."

"I'm sorry, Lena. It's difficult to lose family."

"Thank you. But..." She shifted her gaze to the crowd and blinked away the unshed tears.

"But what?"

"I have no idea why I'm telling you this," she muttered, the words incredulous.

"Maybe because you need to talk about it."

"Maybe." She cleared her throat and fidgeted with her stir stick again. "It's not just that she was family. I mean, she was, of course, but it's more than that." She pushed away her empty glass, the stir stick apparently no longer providing the distraction she needed. "My father left shortly after I was born, and my mother died a year later. My grandma was the only parent I ever had, the only family I've ever known. She was my support system. And now, she's gone."

Lena's loneliness gaped like a black hole, swallowing me into its dark depths. I sucked in a breath at the shock of its intensity and strangled my beer bottle trying to pull myself out of my empathy and back into myself. I finally had her attention, but I hadn't bargained on such a deep emotional connection.

Overwhelmed, I reached for her hand. Her palm was slick with nervous sweat, and as I wrapped my fingers around hers, they quaked. "I am so sorry, Lena. I can't imagine what that must be like. My family means everything to me. But—" I ran my thumb across the back of her hand. "—you're not alone. At least, not right now." I quirked my mouth, hoping the goofy grin would lighten the mood.

Her eyes darted to her hand in mine, and her spine went rigid. She pulled her hand away in a slow, halting movement. "No, I'm not. Thank you for that."

"Anytime. Really. If you want to get another drink sometime or dinner…"

Her eyes widened, and she blinked rapidly, her reaction bordering on panic.

I backpedaled. "Or a swim. My cousin Niko and I swim every day, right around that same place you ran into us earlier. You're welcome to join us any time."

Her shoulders relaxed. "Thanks. We'll see. I have a lot to sort out."

"I'm sure. It's an open invitation. Whenever you're ready."

"Would you two like another drink?" The bartender appeared out of nowhere, and my gut clenched in anticipation of Lena's response.

She shook her head. "No, thank you."

My mood sank, the extent of my disappointment surprising.

"I should probably get going," she said. "I've had a couple and wouldn't want to drive into an alligator pond." Her lips trembled sheepishly, and I adored what it did to her face.

"Definitely don't want that."

She got up and slung her purse over her shoulder. I stood with her but didn't know what to do with my hands—they itched to touch her—so, I shoved them in my pockets.

"Thanks for the chat, Elias. And the song." She tilted her head. "I didn't know how much I needed either."

"Anytime, Lena."

She nodded, gave me a little wave, and walked off toward the parking lot.

I watched her retreating form and tried to tease apart the battle raging inside me. I refused to believe my interest in her stemmed from anything more than needing to indulge my unanswered song. But I'd finally grabbed her attention, and my compulsion still demanded something more.

The sensation was sure to vanish as soon as I soaked up the adoration of the rest of the crowd. I waded through the sea of devoted fans until I found Niko at a table with two women staring at him like he was a celebrity. Perfect. Just what the siren ordered.

"May I join you?" I pulled out a chair and flashed my most charming smile.

The women glanced up and then at each other like they'd just won the lottery.

"Hey, E," Niko said with his Southern drawl. "Just tellin' Melanie and Veronica here about open mic tomorrow night at Coligny. If they bring friends, we might be convinced to sing a couple songs." He smoldered at them with those dark, Mediterranean features of his, and I swear they melted into their chairs.

"Right on," I said and took a seat.

"We wouldn't miss it," one of the women squealed, nearly bouncing out of her seat. "But we don't want to bring friends. We want you all to ourselves."

"Don't worry about that, ladies." Niko leaned back

in his chair and held out both arms. "There's plenty of us to go around."

They devolved into a fit of giggles, and I coughed to cover up a groan. Niko glanced in my direction and winked over his drink. I rolled my eyes. He wasn't usually this brazen. He was laying it on thick, no doubt because he'd seen me talking to Lena and wanted to make a point.

"Y'all want to take a walk on the marina?" Niko asked. "It's beautiful this time of night."

They bounced in their chairs, practically vibrating with excitement, and shared a look for a fraction of a second before blurting, "Absolutely!" and "We'd love that!"

Thank the gods. I couldn't sit there and stomach any more of Niko's ridiculous display.

The brunette looked at me with hopeful eyes. "Will you come, too?"

"Sure. Why not?"

I pushed out of my chair and wondered if Lena made it home safely. Had she had a good time?

My instincts revolted against the unwanted thoughts. What I should have been focusing on was the brunette.

Niko offered an arm to his admirer, and the way she watched him, combined with his above-average interest, he was set for an easy hookup. Hopefully this time he'd follow my advice and leave it at that. They started a slow stroll toward the boardwalk, arm-in-arm.

I turned to the brunette patiently waiting for me with expectant eyes, and something unwelcome unfolded across my chest and clawed its way up my throat. It felt wrong. All I could think about was Lena and her sad eyes and the satisfaction it gave me to make them sparkle with amusement.

I held up a hand and pinched the bridge of my nose with the other, trying to shake off the uncomfortable sensation seizing my body and the war the unwelcome thoughts waged against my siren's compulsion. But the sense of wrongness wouldn't relent.

"Yo! Niko!"

He stopped and glanced back over his shoulder.

"I'm going to head out, man."

Niko's head notched back in surprise, and he spun around to face me. "Really?"

"Yeah. I'm not feeling so hot. I must have eaten something funny."

He frowned, eyes darting to the woman next to me and back. But then his face cracked into the same smug grin from the beach that morning. I wasn't going to hear the end of this tomorrow.

"Nice meeting you," I said to the brunette. "Maybe I'll see you at open mic tomorrow night."

She barely squeaked out a "Yeah" before I spun on my heel and took long, quick strides toward my motorcycle, all the while wondering what had come over me and, more importantly, how I was going to fix it.

CHAPTER SIX
LENA

The next morning, I practiced yoga at the studio in Coligny Square, committed to a new beginning after the fresh outlook I'd gained from listening to Elias the night before. The ninety-minute class delivered, and I left feeling centered and focused.

But the quaint little studio needed some love. The HVAC barely kept the practice room above eighty, the floorboards creaked with every transition to Chaturanga, and I was one of only three students in class. I'd only practiced there a few times in the past, but the sad state of the studio surprised me. I made a mental note to introduce myself to the owner next time I had the chance and ask about the community.

Despite the weak heaters, the island humidity added its own torture to the space, and afterwards I desperately needed to get my body temperature down. I hadn't been in the ocean since I'd arrived on the island, and this seemed like the perfect opportunity. I took a detour on the way back to the house and pedaled my bike to the beach.

I rode through manicured fairways and muddy swamps, past golf carts and tennis courts, under Spanish moss and towering pines. The fragrant air hugged my sweat-soaked skin and sent beads of moisture trailing down my face and back. The island's beauty enveloped my senses, and my grandma felt alive and present in those comforting sensations. I rode along the winding bike paths of Sea Pines toward my beach and drank in the island magic that brought her spirit back to me.

I parked my bike, pulled my sweaty towel out of the basket, and trudged up the sand dune to find a near-empty expanse of beach—everyone must have been at the golf tournament. A single older couple strolled by, hand-in-hand. A brief pang threatened to seize my chest and drag me down, their companionship and devotion a reminder of everything my failed marriage wasn't, but I ruthlessly beat down that line of thinking. Nothing was going to distract me from the beauty of an empty beach and the ocean beyond.

I dropped my towel, kicked off my flip-flops, and peeled off my sweaty tank top and yoga pants. At least I'd worn black panties; they matched my sports bra and kind of made it look like a swimsuit.

The endless ocean glistened so brightly beneath the mid-morning sun, I had to shield my eyes to see anything but glare. And that's when I spotted them —dolphins.

Teenage Lena had been obsessed with dolphins, and I still became giddy anytime they surfaced, especially this close to shore. I stepped toward the water as if those few feet might bring me nearer to them and blinked hard when I realized someone was out there cutting through the water with a rhythmic breast-stroke. Was he... Yes! He was swimming alongside the dolphins as they dipped in and out of the waves.

One of the dolphins raised its head above the surface and clicked. The swimmer slowed, and the dolphin breached the surface. The man stopped and watched it arc. It crashed down sending a wave over his head, and his laugh carried across the distance to the shore. He pushed his hair out of his face, and I instantly recognized him—Elias.

I barked out a surprised laugh, and my hand flew to cover my mouth. He must have heard me, because he swam in a few strokes until he could stand.

"Lena!"

I waved.

He gestured for me to join him. "Come on, Lena!"

Well, I was here for a swim, wasn't I?

I ran through the shore break and duck-dove beneath the waves. The cool water refreshed my hot and sticky skin, and I indulged myself for a moment, submerged in its salty embrace. Then I did my best impression of a dog and paddled toward Elias.

I wasn't a strong swimmer. In fact, what I was

doing could barely pass as swimming, and only if the person was generous. Despite growing up on an island, I hadn't spent a lot of time in the ocean. My grandma and I occasionally visited the beach, but she was afraid of the water, so I never went too deep, and we spent most of our time taking long walks, looking for shells, and building sandcastles. But the water was calm, and Elias seemed like he could swim for both of us. Still, nerves got the best of me, and I stopped short of where he waited and started treading water.

He paddled back with ease, and when he reached me, flipped onto his back and floated atop the waves. "Float with me." His smile brightened the space around him almost as much as the sun off the crystalline water.

I leaned back, allowing the salt water to cradle my body, and my anxiety ebbed.

"Beautiful morning for a swim, isn't it?" he asked.

"Were those dolphins swimming with you?"

"I'd say I was swimming with the dolphins. It's their surf, you know? But yeah. They're here almost every morning. Want to swim with them?"

"What?"

"Do you want to swim with them?" he asked again, this time enunciating each word as if I didn't understand English.

I stared at him in disbelief. Was he crazy?

"Come with me," he said. "If we swim farther out, they'll come back. They love to play in the mornings."

He dove into the water and emerged right next to me with a boyish tilt to his lips. "They like me."

A hysterical laugh escaped me. "You do this often? Swim with dolphins?"

"Sure. Whenever I get the chance. I swim every day, and sometimes we swim the same route." He shrugged a shoulder out of the water; he thought this was the most normal thing in the world. Unbelievable.

He paddled closer and grabbed my hand under the water. My body jerked, surprised by the sudden warmth of his touch and the electric heat it sent down my spine. He wrapped his big hand around mine and squeezed, his blue eyes bright, shimmering with the sun's reflection off the water.

"Come with me." His words slid across my body like smooth silk and pulled me toward him.

"Okay," I replied, hypnotized by his eyes and his voice, my resolve to stay away from charming, handsome men fading into a distant memory. I resumed my slow paddle next to him, luxuriating in the gentle waters under the mid-morning sun.

A splash startled me out of my reverie, and my head snapped to the source. A dolphin's fluke slapped the water only a foot away. My heart pounded in my chest, adrenaline pumping through me in a dizzying rush of shock and fear. I squealed in surprise, my arms flailing as I tried to back away from the wild animal. I inhaled a mouthful of ocean and, coughing and sputtering, still tried to gain distance. Tears and salt water stung my eyes and burned the inside of my nose and throat. My arms ached with effort, and panic set in like a weight atop my pounding chest.

I bumped into something solid and yelped. I spun around, and a strong, muscular arm wrapped around my ribs. Elias. I held onto his shoulders, my body overcome with coughing, and he pulled me close.

"Hey, hey. Lena. It's okay. I've got you. You're okay." He pushed the wet hair clinging to my face out of the way while I coughed up the rest of the ocean. "Surprised you, did he?"

His aquamarine eyes searched mine, and I nodded, trying to regain control over the burn in my windpipe and lungs. I slid my fingers over the smooth skin of his shoulders, the heat of his body warm and safe, and rested my forearms there, clasping my hands behind his neck.

The coughing subsided, and the realization of what I'd done brought awareness back to the rest of my body. My legs brushed against his, my hips pressed against his hard torso, and his thick forearm held me close. Our faces only inches apart, his eyes focused on my mouth. A hot flare of desire shot down my spine and into my core.

I cleared my throat, desperate to break the tension before I did something stupid like maul the gorgeous man holding me with my mouth. I unwrapped my arms from around his neck and pushed the rest of my hair off my face. "Sorry about that. I've never been so close to a wild animal."

He hesitated, his throat bobbing through a slow

swallow, then released me. I felt both relieved and disappointed at his absence. But he remained close enough that his breath still tickled my face, and it made me shiver. His jaw ticked—he was clenching his teeth—his eyes still fixed on my mouth. The idea he felt the same heat that swam through my veins at our touch rekindled the smoldering ember inside me.

"No worries." His words came out rough, and he cleared his throat. "You'll get used to them. Let's go slow. They'll come up alongside us, so don't get spooked. Remember—I'll be right next to you."

Elias set a lazy pace, and I paddled next to him, less fearful now that he was nearby. He'd be there if I needed him.

A dorsal fin breached the water. I started but didn't panic. "There!"

He laughed at my reaction and flipped onto his back, continuing with a backstroke. I regained my composure and resumed paddling.

Two more fins breached the water in tandem, and I stopped again, mouth gaping in awe.

"Come on," Elias urged. "Faster! They want to swim!"

So, I swam. We moved through the water side by side, and three dolphins swam alongside us, all cares left behind in our wake.

The dolphin closest to us disappeared beneath the waves, and I turned onto my side to face Elias and the horizon, hoping it would return.

Without warning, the dolphin sprang from the

water. It sailed over our heads in a dizzying arc, sprinkling us with droplets that glistened like diamonds in the sun. It crashed into the water on its flank with a *thwump*, submerging us beneath a titanic splash.

Elias wiped the water from his face, his muscled shoulders shaking with laughter, his playfulness infectious.

Two fins continued with us along our path, but the third troublemaker stopped and poked its head out of the water, whistling, clicking, and nodding its head. Elias stopped and splashed the dolphin, his brilliant smile shining like the sun, his eyes as bright as the sky.

"Lena! Come here!"

Nervous, but captivated by the beautiful creature bobbing its head above the waves, I swam to meet him, and he wrapped an arm around my waist. "Don't be afraid," he said and pressed me against his muscled torso. Adrenaline surged, but it wasn't just from the wild dolphin within arm's reach.

"Hey, buddy." The dolphin lay on its side, waving a fin in the air as if it understood Elias's words. "Good swim today." He scratched its belly. The dolphin whistled and clicked, waving its fin and nodding its long snout like a dog. "Yeah, you like that, don't you. Go ahead, Lena. Give him a scratch."

My hand shook as I reached out. I touched the dolphin, tentative at first, a brush of my fingertips against its smooth, almost slimy belly. It waved its flipper while I ran my fingers along its slippery skin. I giggled like a child, filled with the indulgent joy of the moment, and scratched in earnest. The dolphin bobbed its head up and down, whistled, and dove beneath the waves. It disappeared for only a moment before launching out of the water in a graceful arc, the sun glinting off its sleek body. It plunged back into the water, sending another wave crashing over our heads.

Joy sprung forth from my heart, a glowing point of light that erupted into a blazing sun, radiating bright, exhilarating energy. I threw my head back in laughter, lost in the moment's decadence. Elias tightened his arm around my waist, and I wrapped mine around his neck. I rested my chin on his shoulder, and he squeezed me tight in his arms.

Peace. Contentment. Happiness. Feelings I hadn't experienced off my mat in what felt like an eternity. They all lived in the space between us.

He pulled back enough to look into my eyes. "See. Nothing to be afraid of."

"Thank you," I said, breathless, but from the dolphins or Elias, I wasn't sure. "Thank you for sharing that with me."

We floated, entwined in each other's arms, faces mere inches apart. The desire in his eyes burned hot, and his gaze once again dipped to my mouth. My eyelids became heavy, each caress of his warm breath against my cool skin sending a luscious frisson of heat to my core. Our lips crept toward each other as if pulled by the force of their hunger to touch.

My body wanted him to kiss me, to press his lips against mine and claim me. But my mind, packed with painful memories of betrayal, won the battle. I leaned in and placed a kiss on his cheek before he could make a move. I lingered there, longer than necessary, desperate to prolong his closeness, but managed enough self-control to pull back. Our eyes locked, and his lips parted in surprise as I wiggled free of his arms and started to swim for the shore.

I made it to shallow waters, scrambled to my feet through the break, and trudged through the sand. Collapsing onto my towel, my breath came hard and heavy. Swimming was not my forte, no matter how fit I was from yoga. I flopped onto my stomach and shielded my eyes from the sun to watch Elias emerge from the water. He strode up the beach, his powerful body moving with purpose, and when he reached me, he sank down onto the sand.

"That was fun." His eyes sparkled in the light, a blue as bright and clear as the ocean in front of us.

I propped myself up on my elbows. "I've never done anything like that." The words tumbled out of me in rapid succession. "That was incredible! I mean, dolphins! We swam with dolphins! In the wild! I can't believe you do that every day."

"Not every day." He leaned back, resting on his elbows, and squinted under the sun's brilliance. "But often enough. There aren't many things I enjoy more than swimming. Sharing a piece of the freedom those dolphins have? Priceless."

I rested my hands on the sand and my chin on my hands, letting the sun warm my body, cool now after the swim and from the light ocean breeze. Elias's eyes bored into my back, so I rolled onto my side and propped my head up on a bent elbow. His eyes shifted to my sports bra, then my underwear, and then my face.

"We need to get you a proper swimsuit if you're going to come swimming with us again."

I sat up and slugged him in the shoulder. "I have a proper swimsuit!"

He mouthed an "ow" and chuckled.

"I hadn't planned on coming this morning. Well, not so early anyway. Yoga was extra hot."

"Ah, yoga. I *knew* you had to be an athlete." His eyes traveled the length of my body before settling back on my face, his hungry gaze as palpable as if he'd used his hands. "You have great muscle tone."

I raised an eyebrow and put every ounce of effort into not blushing, but failed, my insides heating to a boil.

"What? You're in your underwear!"

I swatted at him, and he chuckled again. "I'm serious! I noticed your arms the other day. You don't get arms like that unless you're an athlete."

"Thanks."

I did my own once-over of his magnificent body. *Woof.* "You're not exactly a slouch yourself." He shrugged like that was obvious, and I snorted at his ego.

"So, you do yoga?"

"I do. I'm an instructor. I own a studio in Charleston."

"An athlete and a business owner? Right on."

My pride swelled. "Thanks. It's a lot of work, but it's rewarding. And I love teaching."

"Must be nice to take some time off and be a student for a change."

"It is, I guess. I hadn't thought about it that way, but yeah." Thinking about this as a break to enjoy my own practice hadn't even occurred to me. I used to be like Elias, focusing on positivity and fun in any situation. When had I lost that?

"What about you? You mentioned last night you're not a musician. So, what do you do?"

"I help run the family business. I teach swimming, open diving, sailing, water sports. I run charters. Basically, anything that involves the ocean."

"That sounds very you."

"It is. A new adventure every day. I never know what the next week will bring, but I always know I'll be on the water."

I hesitated, worried that asking about his family might reopen wounds and cause me to spiral, but I was too intrigued not to ask. "You work with your family?"

"Yeah. My family owns the Ocean Explorers Club here in Sea Pines. My papa and his brother started a fishing company when they emigrated from Greece. Then my dad and Niko's dad turned it into what it is today—a tourism company. Charter sailing, open diving, general water sports."

That explained Elias and Niko—their names, their Mediterranean tans, their piercing blue eyes.

"I can't believe your family owns the Ocean Explorers Club. My grandma used to take me on the dolphin cruises when I was little."

"Right on. We still do those, and a lot more. It's funny we both grew up on this island and never met until now."

I couldn't help the mischievous grin that took over my face. "Well, I do think you're a few years older than me." He snorted and rolled his eyes. "But maybe not so surprising. I went to Montessori until high school and spent most of my summers with my grandma at her herbalism shop learning about Ayurveda and natural healing. I'm sure you spent your summers on the water."

"Yup. Helping the family business as soon as I was useful. And I went to high school in Greece, so..."

"Ah. There you go.

"I envy you having such a big family and getting to work with your parents on your family's legacy."

"I'm lucky, for sure. But our parents are much older now and largely out of the day-to-day business. Niko manages the office, the finances, all that stuff." Elias made a face like he tasted something sour. "And I run the charters and classes. With the help of a few of my cousins, of course. Everyone chips in.

"Like I said last night—my family means the world to me. My family and the ocean."

He turned his gaze to the water, and his eyes filled with longing. If Elias ever looked at a woman like that, she'd be lost to him forever.

I propped myself up to sit, bent my legs, and wiggled my toes in the sand. I rested my forearms on my knees and clasped my hands in front of me. Elias scooched forward, and we sat side by side in comfortable silence, watching the never-ending expanse of ocean perform its slow, rhythmic dance.

"Whatcha thinking?"

"About my studio," I said, wistfully.

Out of the corner of my eye, he tilted his head to face me, patiently waiting for an explanation. A good listener, too. Great. The reasons for resisting a friendship with this man were dwindling fast.

"It's silly." I looked down at my feet, embarrassed and wishing I hadn't said anything. But his eyes remained steady and penetrating, and I sighed in concession, resting my cheek on my hands to look at him. "Your family business. It sounds like a community, everyone doing their part and supporting each other. Everyone's needed.

"The way things are going with my studio right now, I'm not sure it needs me anymore. Candace—my office manager—she runs such a tight ship. And we have enough instructors even without me there. Losing my only family, not feeling like I'm needed at my own studio..."

My husband leaving me for another woman.
"I want to feel like I belong. Like I'm needed."
Like I'm important to someone. Like I'm loved.
"And right now, I just feel alone."

CHAPTER SEVEN
ELIAS

Sadness wound around Lena's words and emotions. The swimming and the dolphins had lifted her mood, and her genuine happiness had brightened an already luminous day. But that persistent sadness had returned, tunneling through her contentment to steal her joy. I needed to bring her back.

"I mean, you *could* look at it like that."

"I'm not sure how else to look at it."

"Really?" My head jerked back in surprise. "Lena, *you're* the reason the studio exists. You created that community. You're the reason the business runs so smoothly. *You* did that. No one else." I shrugged; her success seemed so obvious to me. "I don't know. Sounds to me like you're needed."

She swallowed, and her eyes became wide and glassy, appreciation and something bordering on affection replacing the breakthrough sadness I'd sensed moments ago. Good.

"I did do that, didn't I?" She sounded mystified by the realization.

"You sure did. And if they don't need you looking over their shoulder every minute of every day? That's a testament to the foundation you built."

"Yo! E!"

My head snapped up to the source of the deep voice that severed our moment like a guillotine. Niko jogged toward us in trunks and wet hair. He stopped in front of us, hands on hips. "Hey, man. What's doin'?"

"Hey, Niko. You remember Lena?"

"A pleasure, Lena. I'm Elias's better-looking cousin, Niko."

What an ass. I scowled at him, and he winked.

Lena bit her lip, suppressing a laugh. "Hi, Niko. Nice to meet you."

"We were just drying off from a swim," I said. "What's up?"

"It's gettin' late, and I figured you'd need a reminder—you've got a fishing charter this afternoon."

"Ah, shit, that's right." I grimaced. "Sorry, Lena. Duty calls."

I hopped to my feet and held out a hand. She took it, and I pulled her up, not wanting to let go of her hand or our time together.

"No problem. I need to get back anyway." She brushed the sand from her legs. "Paperwork."

I made a face, and she laughed.

I needed an excuse to make her laugh like that again. I licked my lips, my mind working through the possibilities. "Listen. You seemed uncomfortable in the water today."

She snorted, and it was the most adorable sound I'd ever heard. "Understatement."

"Why don't you let me teach you how to swim? The basics. You'll feel more comfortable in the water, and I'll feel more comfortable knowing you're not going to inhale half the ocean next time you get startled."

She rolled her eyes, but then nodded, a shy turn of her mouth blessing her pouty lips. "I'd like that. Thank you."

"Great. Call the Ocean Explorers Club and leave your number with the front desk. I'll text you when I get to work."

"Sounds good." She picked up her towel, sweaty yoga clothes, and sandals. "Thanks for the swim. It was... memorable." The corner of her mouth turned up as if we shared a secret. "See you soon, Elias. Nice meeting you, Niko."

"Bye," I said and watched her head for the dunes.

Niko clapped me on the shoulder, and I jumped. "Well, well, well." I didn't need to see his face to know he sported his smug grin. "How the mighty have fallen."

"Shut it, Niko."

He doubled over laughing—so dramatic. I spun

away from him and marched toward the house. He jogged up next to me, but before he could add any more annoying commentary, I tried to make sure he understood the score. "I'm serious, man. She just needs help with swimming. She nearly drowned today, and I can't have that on my conscience."

"Uh-huh." His raised eyebrows and drawn-out, sarcastic tone told me he wasn't buying it. I didn't blame him; I wasn't entirely convinced myself. Truth was, after today, I wanted to get to know Lena. She intrigued me. Passionate about health and fitness, an entrepreneur, easy to talk to and not at all clingy—thank the gods—we connected on so many levels. Not to mention she was sexy as hell.

I wanted to know everything about her. Where had she traveled? How had she come to own a yoga studio? What did she do for fun? I had an overwhelming urge to comfort her, soothe her loneliness, and provide her with the friendship and connection she so desperately missed from her life. Help her feel like she belonged.

Panic tightened around my neck like a noose. That string of thoughts sounded like Niko, not me. I didn't want to tether myself to a single person. She may not be clingy now, but I knew from experience how women could get in a relationship. I refused to let anyone put a box around my life, limit my freedom, and bind me with expectation. No way. I needed my independence. The ocean was my home, as vast and wide as life's possibilities, and no relationship could ever replace its wonders.

But the beast caged in my chest stirred again and demanded attention. I glanced over my shoulder. In the distance, Lena descended from the top of the dune into the tree-cover, and all I could think about was when I'd get to see her again.

CHAPTER EIGHT
LENA

The next week sailed by in a flurry of meetings, lawyers, banks, and paperwork. By Saturday night, I was looking forward to a lazy Sunday free of responsibility and a long swim with the charming instructor whose magnetic voice, athletic body, and carefree personality was becoming harder to resist with each lesson. Dawn splayed its fingers over the horizon as I pedaled my way into Harbour Town, and the early morning's quiet stillness delivered the peace and tranquility I'd hoped for.

I locked my beach cruiser to the bike rack in front of the breakfast joint my grandma and I had frequented since I was a child. I hadn't visited the spot yet on this trip, scared the experience might trigger further heartache and grief. But as I climbed the creaky steps of the familiar wooden porch, the weight atop my shoulders didn't become any heavier, and the aching hole in my heart didn't expand.

The touch of the cool, damp air against my skin, the island smells swirling together with coffee and bakery, the whine and whirr of the espresso machine... Memories surfaced, and instead of pain and loss, nostalgia and reminiscence conjured a sense of comfort and home.

But the real test waited inside.

I pushed through the front door into a near-empty café, and the owner—my grandma's closest friend—looked up from the register. Her eyes went wide, and I smiled. "Hi, Sonia."

"Lena! Oh, Lena, my dear."

The older woman with kind eyes, dark, wrinkled skin, and a motherly mien walked around the counter and opened her arms. I stepped into them, and she wrapped me in a warm hug. Her perfume's floral scent and the softness of her loving embrace brought me to tears, and a single sob escaped me as they spilled down my face. I squeezed harder, relieved my emotions stemmed from happiness instead of grief. I'd missed Sonia, and her presence and our connection amplified my sense of home.

"My beautiful girl." She pulled back and held me at arm's length. "I was wondering when you'd come by. If you'd waited much longer, I'd have come knocking on your door." She chuckled and pulled me back into her arms.

"I'm sorry. I should have come sooner, but..."

She released me again and held my hands in her knobby fingers. "No sorries, hun. I miss your grandma terribly. I can only imagine how difficult this must be for you. You needed time, and that's perfectly fine. Now. What can I get you for breakfast while we catch up?"

"Just a triple latte for now, thanks."

"Still over-caffeinating?"

I laughed. "Yes. Grandma never could break me of the habit."

"Bah!" She waved a hand and walked behind the counter to the espresso machine. "There's nothing wrong with coffee. Your grandma just had a *thing* about caffeine."

"But a glass of brandy or two was okay." I chuckled and shook my head.

"We all have our vices. So. Tell me. What have you been up to?"

I leaned against the counter and watched her pack coffee into the portafilter. "Paperwork. Sorting through an entire life's worth of stuff. Deciding what to keep, what to donate."

"Oh, honey. I'm so sorry."

I shook my hand at her like there was an insect in front of me. "Don't. Please don't. I can't take the pity voice. Especially not from you. I'll just start spiraling."

"No pity voice. Got it." She nodded and returned her attention to steaming my milk.

"I've been taking swimming lessons."

"Really?"

"Yeah. I've had two so far, but I'm already more comfortable in the water."

"Your grandma hated the water, but I always thought she should've gotten you lessons."

"No time like the present. And focusing on something new has been helping me stay positive." But it wasn't just the swimming that had lifted my mood. It was Elias. His positive attitude was infectious, and his lighthearted outlook had softened the impending sense of doom that gripped my insides anytime I considered my future.

"That's wonderful!"

She handed me the paper cup with a plastic lid, and I blew on the little spout as I brought the divine goodness to my lips. I closed my eyes and sipped. "Mmm. Liquid perfection. Thanks, Sonia."

"You're welcome, hun. Just glad you're here."

My phone vibrated. Who could be calling this early?

I fished my phone out of my purse, hoping nothing was wrong with the studio, but it wasn't Candy. I didn't recognize the number, but it had a Hilton Head area code, so I answered.

"Hello?"

"Lena?"

"Speaking."

"This is Harry. From Hot Yoga Hilton Head? We spoke last week?"

"Oh, yes! Harry! Hello."

I'd introduced myself to Harry after class earlier in the week and discovered the reasons behind the state of the studio. Two instructors had moved off the island the previous year, and he hadn't been able to find replacements. Membership had dwindled with the new, limited schedule, and maintenance became an expense he couldn't afford. He desperately wanted to retire but felt he owed it to the community to stay open.

I empathized with his situation—I would have done the same—so, I'd given him my number and told him if he needed help while I was in town, I'd be happy to oblige. Apparently, he needed help.

"I hate to ask on such short notice, but can you cover my 8:30? I need to take my dog to the vet, and I can't get ahold of my other teachers. I'm really worried. She's never *not* gotten up for her morning walk, and—"

"Stop right there, Harry. I'll take care of it, no problem."

He let out a tremendous sigh. "I owe you big time. I'm taking her in now. I'll leave a set of keys in the mailbox. The HVAC controls are behind the front desk, and the room takes a while to heat up so—"

"Don't worry. I'll figure it out. You go take care of your dog."

"Thank you so much, Lena."

"No problem."

I ended the call and checked the time—ten after seven. If I was going to make it to Coligny in time to prepare the practice room before class, I needed to move. But first I needed to text Elias.

Hey. I just got a call from the yoga
studio. They need a sub for the 8:30,
so I won't make our swim lesson.
Sorry for the short notice.

I tucked my phone back in my purse. "Sorry, Sonia. That was the yoga studio in Coligny. They need a teacher at 8:30."

"Go, go. I know how much you love teaching. Just promise you'll come back and see me soon?"

"Absolutely. Promise."

I leaned across the counter, kissed her wrinkled cheek, and an hour later turned on the heat of Hot Yoga Hilton Head for a ninety-minute flow.

I lit a stick of Nag Champa and put it in the incense holder, grabbed a rental mat and towel for myself, and set up my space in the practice room. Two students entered and set up their mats for quiet meditation.

I returned to the foyer to grab a bottle of water, and the studio door swung open. Elias walked in wearing swim trunks, a muscle tank, and his crooked smile. I laughed aloud at the sight, and he winked at me before peeling the plastic off a mat he'd clearly bought on his way over.

"What are you doing here?"

"Taking a yoga class."

I rolled my eyes and chuckled. "I can see that."

He stepped forward to meet me. "Yoga's important to you. It makes you happy. Your face lights up when you talk about it." He shrugged. "I wanted to see you shine."

My heart swelled, and the walls I'd erected around it started to crumble. Nervous, I tucked my hair behind my ear and cleared my throat. "Let's get you set up then."

I grabbed a towel and showed him into the practice room. While he rolled out his mat, I brought over a couple of blocks and a strap and set them at the top of his space. He scowled at the props. "What are those for?"

"They're to help you maintain alignment in certain poses. If you need them."

He stared at the props a beat longer, then turned his furrowed brow to me.

"Don't worry. I'll let you know when and how to use them if you need to modify. You know the basics, right? Downward Dog, Upward Dog, Warrior One..."

"Yeah, I think so." He shoved a hand through his hair. "Sounds familiar."

"You'll be fine. Just watch me. And take it at your own pace. If something doesn't feel right, don't do it." I eyed his muscle tank. "You might want to lose the shirt. It's going to get in the way, and you're just going to sweat through it anyway."

He raised an eyebrow, and his lips shaped into a mischievous smile.

I rolled my eyes and shoved the towel into his chest. Time to get started.

For someone who didn't practice regularly, or at all, Elias wasn't half bad. I shouldn't have been surprised. He was an athlete, and his base level of fitness showed in his flow. His balance and flexibility needed work, but he could hold a pose and wasn't too shabby for a beginner.

We had that in common, a passion for movement and a deep connection to our bodies. Watching Elias swim, anyone could see he belonged in the water. It amplified his playful nature, making his spirit shine even brighter. It reminded me of how I transformed when I stepped onto my mat—present and carefree.

And he'd wanted to see me in that same light. Elias had shown up. For me. My heart expanded with affection, knocking down another piece of that crumbling wall. Maybe he wasn't the playboy I'd imagined.

At the end of class, one of the students approached me and asked for help with her Eagle pose. I stole a glance at Elias, tilted my head toward the student, and gave a little wave. As much as I was dying to know what he thought of class, my students came first.

I spent the next fifteen minutes helping the young woman with proper alignment. I'd noticed during class she'd struggled to stay upright in the pose, losing her balance and tipping forward. I immediately saw the problem—she was collapsing into her back and not pulling up through her core—and as soon as I corrected her form, she was flying high. She attacked me with a big, sweaty hug and an outburst of thanks, then pumped her fists in the air while leaving the studio.

Gratification wrapped its arms around me as I

turned off the heat and closed up the practice room. Helping bring the joy of yoga to others was why I loved teaching, and the morning's unexpected class had been a welcome reminder.

Refreshed and fulfilled, I locked the studio, turned toward the parking lot, and nearly choked on my breath. Elias leaned against a motorcycle, ankles crossed, thick arms folded over the muscle tank now clinging to his sweaty chest. He flashed his easy, crooked smile, and I thought my knees might give out.

He ran a hand through his sweaty hair. "Hi."

I swallowed, attempting to regain composure. "Hi." I stepped to meet him. "You did great today."

"Really? I felt like I had two left legs. Yoga is no joke."

"Really. You have excellent awareness of your body and space. Once you get the hang of the flow, you'll be able to tailor the poses for yourself, and that's when the magic happens."

"You're an awesome teacher, Lena."

My heart burst with pride. "Thank you."

"I can see why your studio in Charleston is so successful. There was a sense of community in there, even with just the four of us. It felt like we were all working together."

"Thanks. That's kind of you."

"It's true. I know you said you don't feel needed, but what I experienced in class today says different. You've been here for what—two weeks? And the owner already trusts you enough to ask for your help? That student needed you after class, and I definitely needed you to help me with those bricks."

I bit the inside of my cheek to hold back a snicker. "Blocks."

"See?"

I chuckled despite myself.

He pressed on. "You're needed. This community needs you, and I wanted to make sure you recognized that."

"Thanks." I tucked a loose hair behind my ear, embarrassed by the praise, but grateful for the perspective. "Thanks for reminding me."

"Anytime." He met my gaze with the full force of his Hollywood smile, sending butterflies to assault my insides. He pushed off the bike and put on his helmet. "I gotta jet—big charter this afternoon. I'll see you Tuesday morning for our lesson?"

"I'll be there."

"Right on." He hopped on his motorcycle, and the thunder of the engine tore through the morning silence. "Later, Lena," he shouted and sped off.

The rumble of Elias's bike faded as I unlocked my beach cruiser and tossed my things in the basket. I hopped on and started the long pedal back to the south end of Sea Pines. The breeze felt cool against my heated skin, and the Sunday morning tranquility soon swept me into reflection.

The island's mystic energy surrounded me, and Elias, Sonia, and my grandma's ever-present spirit had started to fill the gaping hole in my heart with joy, beauty, and comfort. I no longer cried every day. I could think straight. I could finally consider my future.

A crane spread its wings and launched out of the swampy waterway. The stream opened into one of the larger ponds, and an alligator sun-bathed on the bank, gaping jaws parted and turned up to the late-morning sun. I smiled. First gator of the trip.

Gods, I loved Hilton Head. So peaceful. So magical. So me.

But I needed to get back to my community, didn't I? Back to my studio and students. Teaching that class and Elias's wise words had made that abundantly clear.

But the more I thought about it, in many respects, my life in Charleston had come to an end. I didn't have a house or a family to go back to. My so-called "friends" belonged to my ex. All I had left was my studio, which, if I was honest, had been tainted by sharing it with my ex-husband and discovering he'd cheated on me with one of our students. For years. Angry heat seared my neck, and I quickly pushed the memory away.

Maybe it was time to start over. I'd told Elias the Charleston studio could practically run itself, and I hadn't been exaggerating; no reason I couldn't hand off the reins. I'd built that community from scratch; no reason I couldn't do that again somewhere else.

Was it possible? Could I do that?

I didn't want to live in the past, but Hilton Head no

longer felt like a step backward. Instead, my grandma's house and the island felt fresh as if old loves and distant memories had been reawakened with a new twist. For the first time since I'd arrived, I pictured what the future might look like if I stayed on the island, and I liked what I saw.

CHAPTER NINE
LENA

Another week passed, and the woman staring back at me in the bathroom mirror Saturday night looked different than I remembered her. The weather had turned warmer, and with all the time I spent at the beach, my reflection had a tan and an explosion of freckles. Sun-bleached hair tumbled in waves across bare shoulders above a strapless sundress, the pale blonde stark against browned skin tinted with sunburn. Grey eyes, no longer filled with despair, looked bright beneath mascara-darkened eyelashes.

My stomach flipped. This was a terrible idea.

I'd run into Elias on the beach earlier that morning after his swim. Distracted by the water droplets trailing down the planes of his hard body and lulled into acquiescence by his seductive voice, my brain short-circuited. He asked if I had plans, and before my brain could connect with my mouth, I said no.

"There's a full moon tonight. I thought I'd grab a bottle of wine and we could take it down to the beach. The ocean looks magical in the moonlight."

The words sounded in my head throughout the day, a hypnotic repetition as I went about my business.

Goosebumps pebbled my skin, the anticipation of our first date a terrifying excitement. The insidious villain of doubt poked holes in my assessment of his sincere interest and genuine nature, a vestige of the damage my ex-husband had wrought on my ability to trust. But despite my misgivings, I felt as though I *couldn't* deny him.

The old stories about sirens resurfaced, Elias's mesmerizing voice and the force it exerted over my attention persuading me to consider the uncanny possibility.

The doorbell interrupted my musings and sent a rush of adrenaline through my body. I examined myself in the mirror one last time, then squinted to meet my eyes in harsh appraisal.

"Don't do stupid shit, Lena."

I nodded at my reflection and walked to the door.

Elias stood on the porch carrying a basket in the crook of his arm, the neck of a wine bottle poking out the top. The porch light glinted off his sandy blond hair, and his blue eyes and straight white teeth gleamed against his tanned skin. The sleeves of his linen shirt were pushed up and hung untucked over loose, khaki pants. With his Birkenstocks, he'd gone full beach bum, and it suited him. Lust merged with the adrenaline and set my body aflame with desire. *Cool it, Lena.*

"Hi, gorgeous," he said.

My chest fluttered from the silk in his voice. He leaned across the threshold and pecked my cheek, his closeness filling my senses with warmth, coconut, and sandalwood. How I didn't melt into a pile of goo was beyond me, but I reminded myself what happened the last time I let my body succumb to unrelenting hotness, and it tempered my runaway lust.

"Hi."

"You ready?"

"Absolutely."

He held out his arm. I took it and stepped out onto the porch. The door clicked shut behind us. No going back now.

We strolled along the winding path, making small talk under the light of the full moon shining through the canopy. We crested the ridge of the dune, and my lips parted on an intake at the breathtaking vista.

The full moon hung in the sky, a lambent globe swollen from perspective and bursting with light and warmth. It illuminated the night as if the sun handed over its baton, casting an ethereal glow across the water and turning the ocean into an unending expanse of liquid crystal.

"You weren't kidding," I muttered and tore my eyes away from the spectacular scene to face him. "It's beautiful."

He met my gaze, eyes sparkling like the water in the moonlight. "I thought you'd enjoy this. Come on." He took my hand and led me farther down the beach. Overcome by the beauty of nature and the warmth of his touch, I interlaced my fingers with his and squeezed. He glanced down and smiled.

We reached the water's edge just shy of the waves before he set down the basket, pulled out a blanket, and spread it across the sand. "Have a seat. I'll open the wine."

His gallantry made my chest flutter. I hadn't dated since... since I'd met my ex-husband.

After the divorce, I'd avoided men like kids avoided broccoli. The damaged part of my heart tried to protect itself, reminding me that Elias's entire schtick had to be an act. But I'd gotten to know him over the past couple of weeks, and my cynicism couldn't hold out against his genuine nature. His authenticity forced me to consider another option—that his thoughtfulness was sincere, and his intentions were honorable. My inner romantic resurfaced and begged me to allow the handsome man pouring two glasses of expensive Chardonnay to sweep me off my feet.

I kicked off my sandals, sat on the blanket, and extended my legs, reclining on my hands to watch the moonlight dance across the waves. He handed me a glass and raised his own, holding me captive with the bottomless depths of his ocean eyes. "To new beginnings."

"To new beginnings."

We clinked glasses, and a slow smile stole possession of my face even as I drank. This man was far too charming. He lay on his side and propped himself up on one elbow, one knee bent, wine glass loose in his hand. He looked like a modern Adonis, his tanned Greek features stark against the white and khaki linen reflecting the moon's soft glow.

"How's everything with the house?" he asked. "We haven't talked about it since the first day we met."

"No, I suppose we haven't." I shifted onto my side to face him, leaning on one arm and holding my wine in the other. "Which has been nice, by the way. Our lessons give me a chance to take my mind off all that. Focus on something else." I sipped my wine. "But, to answer your question, the paperwork is done. My grandmother's property, including the house, is now in my name."

"Congratulations."

"Huh." I blinked. Congratulations struck me as odd. "I hadn't looked at it that way."

"What way?"

"Something deserving of congratulations." I breathed deep through my nose, considering the idea, then deflated like a balloon. "I guess I still think of inheriting an empty house as part of losing my grandma."

He looked over his shoulder at the ocean and nodded slightly. "I can see that." He sipped his wine. "But I also see it as an accomplishment. It's difficult to deal with paperwork when you're *not* struggling with loss. I avoid it myself. Toxic stuff." He scrunched up his face and feigned a shudder. I chuckled at his near-visceral reaction to responsibility. "But dealing with paperwork after what you've been through?" He shook his head. "I don't know how you did it. It hasn't even been a month. The way I see it, that's grounds for congratulations."

He was right, of course. As usual. This wasn't the first time Elias had shined a flashlight on my glass-half-empty takes.

Under the weight of my grief, my thoughts had focused on what I no longer had instead of the potential for possibility. Elias had pointed it out enough times it was clear I needed to shift my thinking and turn around my negative headspace. Now, with some of the deepest sadness lifted, that finally seemed possible.

"Thank you. For the congratulations and the perspective. Apparently, you came into my life to remind me of possibility." I held up my glass. He clinked his against it, and we both drank. "But, yeah, it's a big weight off. No more lawyers."

Puh, he grunted. "Lawyers. Even worse than paperwork." He tipped his glass in my direction and took another deep drink.

I huffed out a chuckle. "Why am I not surprised you hate lawyers?"

He shrugged. "My live-and-let-live personality?" He flashed his white teeth and waggled his eyebrows, making me laugh in earnest.

"That might have something to do with it."

"What can I say? I value my freedom." His gaze returned to the ocean as if pulled there by magnets. "I love the ocean. Its vastness. Its endless possibilities. So much to experience and explore. No boundaries. Just a horizon full of promise."

"You don't want to be tied down by anything."

"No, I don't. I'll always be there for my family—that will never change—but aside from them? I want to live by my own rules, not someone else's expectations. Or commentary." He said the last word dryly and rolled his eyes, evoking another huff of laughter. "I want to take off at a moment's notice on a new adventure, experience a new challenge. I want to ride the wave of life without worrying about other people wiping out."

"No one is *that* free. What you're describing sounds like a dream."

He gave me a sidelong glance, his features contorting like I spoke a language he didn't comprehend.

The corner of my mouth climbed at his reaction; he really didn't understand. "You have to live somewhere. Eat. Sleep. Provide for yourself. Which means you have to have a job."

"Sure, but nothing's permanent. You can always find a path to more freedom."

"That's very idealistic of you."

"I'm an idealistic guy. It's been true so far in my

life, and I've been on this wild ride for forty-five years. But back to you…"

He held his glass to his lips and stared at me with intent under raised eyebrows until I took the hint and drank with him. The buttery California vintage was delicious, hardly a burden.

"If you're done with all the paperwork and lawyers, why are you still here? Aren't you eager to get back to Charleston?"

"Hm," I grunted and stared into my wine. "You'd think that." I swirled the golden goodness in my glass, brought it under my nose, and inhaled its delicious aroma. I regarded Elias, his curious eyes waiting for my reply. "No." I shook my head. "I'm not eager to get back."

"What about your studio?"

"You were right the other day—what you said about me being the reason it runs so smoothly. *I* made that happen, and I'm proud of that. But aside from teacher training, Candace can run the studio herself. And it's time I let her.

"It's time for me to move on from my past, and my past is in Charleston. I need to start something new. I need to start over." I averted my eyes to the wine, unable to hold Elias's penetrating stare while I vocalized the plans I'd only solidified that morning. "I want to expand Yoga Star. I want to open a studio here in Hilton Head. I want to move back to the island."

The words rolled off my tongue far easier than I'd thought possible. They tasted right as they passed my lips, natural, as if the universe yearned to hear them. And in that moment, I knew that's what my soul craved—to stay here and build a new life.

The waves punctuated the silence. I looked up, and Elias's eyes moved through a slow blink, his mouth slightly agape. He closed his lips into a set line and swallowed.

CHAPTER TEN
ELIAS

Her grey eyes caught the moonlight, staring at me expectantly, a nervous hopefulness apparent in the twitch of her mouth. A cacophony of thoughts swirled through my brain, and the thing that had been beating against my chest for weeks redoubled its efforts. I gulped my wine, trying to pull myself together.

"You're surprised," she said, a shy observation, hesitant with fear of judgment or need for encouragement, it was hard to tell. I was too preoccupied by what it might mean if she stayed. My heart rate ticked up at the idea.

"I'm sorry. You caught me off guard. I *was* surprised, but not in a bad way. Expanding your business is a fantastic idea. And you already have a house." The words sounded placating even to my own ears, and I hoped she didn't pick up on my sudden unease.

"Thanks." She beamed, her face alight with pride

and hope, making her even more beautiful in the moonlight.

I exhaled, the confusion in my head falling away at the sight of her radiant smile. "You're so beautiful, Lena."

She lowered her eyes and tucked hair behind her ear.

She'd done that before, anytime she felt embarrassed or moments became too intimate. But I wanted her to acknowledge the truth. I took her chin between my forefinger and thumb, and tilted her head until she met my eyes. "Especially when you do that."

"Do what?"

"Smile. Really smile. From the inside. I remember the first time it happened."

I released her chin but held her gaze, her grey eyes sparkling with surprise and curiosity.

"The first time we swam together. With the dolphins. Your entire energy transformed. Your face lit up. I remember thinking I wanted to do whatever I could to keep you smiling."

The ocean breeze blew loose strands of moonlit hair across her freckled face, and she tucked them away. "It's easy to smile around you, Elias. You have this... presence about you. This passion for life. It's contagious. When I'm around you, I remember how wonderful life can be. How life used to be.

"I think I used to be like you. Living life to the fullest. Excited by each new moment, each new adventure. By nature and connection." She looked out at the ocean. "And then life happened. So much betrayal and hurt and loss. All at once. And this heaviness settled over everything."

The wind gusted, and she closed her eyes. I sat quietly, allowing her a moment to simply be and feel, to soak in her realizations and the beauty surrounding her, because I'd sensed her emotions transforming over the past week. Even though she described her pain, a distance separated her feelings from her understanding of them, and that separation had lightened her emotional burden.

She turned back to me, and those little wisps of moonlight floated around her face. My chest tightened and my fingers flexed, the urge to reach out and take her into my arms overwhelming. But she needed to finish.

"And then I came back to the island. I came home." She wrapped her arms around herself, and contentment replaced the last vestiges of sorrow and heartbreak. "This has always been home. I resisted it at first —the house felt so empty, so hollow. But my grandma's spirit is still there. It's a part of the house, a part of the island. It's in my memories. And there's comfort in that. I'm not sure I want to let that go.

"Life is peaceful here. And I desperately need peace. I think it's time for me to start over. Here."

Her energy lifted. She'd fallen back in love with the island, and I had no doubt its magic would heal the remaining wounds to her soul.

The song I sang to her that first night we talked

sprang into my head. I couldn't stop myself; my power surged.

Pleasures be waiting by the sea
with a smile for all the world to see.

The notes spilled out of me, threaded with my siren's power, drawing her in as effortlessly as the words connected with her hope.

She sat transfixed, eyes wide, lips parted, breath quickening.

The beast in my chest exploded from its cage, refusing to be ignored, and in a moment of clarity, I finally knew its name—feelings. *My* feelings. For Lena. Tenderness. Affection. Desire. All for the radiant and resilient woman sitting across from me. I needed her in my arms; the beast of my emotions refused to be caged any longer.

I sat up and moved to where she sat cross-legged on the blanket. I reached across the remaining distance between us and brushed the wisps of hair from her face, lightly trailing my fingertips along her cheekbone. She leaned into my touch, and the air between us crackled with anticipation. Her eyelids shuttered, and gooseflesh pebbled her naked shoulders. The feel of her skin and her body's reaction made me harden with need and shattered my resolve. I leaned in and took her bottom lip between mine.

She tasted of Chardonnay and vanilla lip gloss, and her plump, silky lip between mine destroyed rational thought. I wrapped an arm around her waist and pulled her into me. She gripped my shoulders with delicate yet strong hands and squeezed, urging me closer. Desire surged, and my body reacted on instinct, wanting more, wanting to possess her. I parted her lips with my tongue and ran it along her top and bottom lip before taking her mouth.

My body hardened, aching with need, and my gentle kisses quickly turned passionate and hungry. I lay back and pulled Lena down with me, one leg draped over my hips. She slid a hand into the opening at the top of my shirt, and my skin burned under her touch. I wanted to rip our clothes off and feel that sensation across my entire body.

She pulled back, and I thought I'd lose my mind. Her fingers danced across my chest, and I ran my hand up and down her back. She stared down at me, lips swollen, cheeks flushed, searching my face as if she wasn't sure how she'd gotten there, but also as if she never wanted to leave. She shifted her weight, wedging my leg tight between hers, and kissed me wildly, devouring my mouth with a hunger matching my own.

My emotions stirred, evolving into something far deeper than affection and desire. And although the feelings unnerved me, they didn't deter my intent. I wanted her. Here. Now. I pulled her fully atop me and pressed my hips into hers. I wanted her to feel how hard she made me.

She whimpered, and I lost control. I dragged her

sundress down below her breasts and thumbed her nipple. She groaned, and my breath quickened and cock twitched in response to her throaty reaction.

I released her breast and ran my hand up her firm, muscular thigh. My hands clenched when I reached the ass I'd been staring at for weeks. I squeezed, hard, and rocked her against my cock.

I slid her thong to the side and found her impossibly wet. I ran my knuckle along her seam, up and down, and her hips moved with the rhythm of my hand. She let out a strangled sigh and propped her leg up, silently asking for more. I sunk two fingers into her warm depths, and she moaned with pleasure.

I alternated flicking her clit and delving my fingers into her warmth, and she trailed hers down my torso to the waistband of my pants. She took the lobe of my ear in between her teeth and tugged. The shot of pain sent a fresh jolt of desire straight to my cock.

"I want to feel you." The words left her lips in a breathy whisper, and I shivered as they caressed my ear.

My fingers slowed when she tugged my pants down over my hips, distracted by the idea of her holding me. She pushed them down to my knees and slid her hand inside my boxers. I jerked at the gentle touch of her fingers on my sensitive flesh, and when she moved her thumb over the wetness at the tip, I grunted like a hungry animal.

I flipped her onto her back and ripped the tiny piece of fabric from her body. I palmed her clit while I fucked her with my fingers. She took my cock and pumped in a slow, steady rhythm, her hand wrapped around it in a firm, unyielding grip. I didn't know how long I could last, her unrelenting strokes maddening.

She thrust her hips toward me, matching my rhythm, and gripped me tighter. I was going to come, pleasure building furiously at the base of my spine. It begged for release, so I pressed my thumb over her throbbing clit in faster, harder strokes.

"Come with me, Lena."

She moaned, deep and throaty, and it nearly sent me over the edge.

"Come with me, baby."

Her responsive body didn't disappoint. She stiffened then trembled, seizing around my fingers and crying out with each pulse of pleasure. And with the next stroke of her hand, I came. Hot waves of come shot from me, my hips rigid through my orgasm.

I collapsed atop her, careful not to crush her beneath my weight. We lay there for a moment, panting, spent, and satisfied.

I pressed up onto my forearms. She was so beautiful, face luminous and flushed from sex, and she looked at me as if I was a hero.

Those beastly feelings returned with a vengeance, expanding out of my chest to conquer my soul. Panic rose to meet the tenderness, and I swallowed, an overpowering need to escape kidnapping rational thought. My brain went wild with impressions of an imaginary future. Burying myself inside her in my bed. Watching her fall asleep after we made love. Waking up each morning with her in my arms.

Panic consumed me, and I froze.

Lights flickered to my right, and my head snapped up. Two flashlights. A dog barked. "Shit."

I rolled off Lena, and we both scrambled to our feet. I grabbed a towel to wipe us off and pulled up my pants. She righted her dress, smoothed out her hair, and cleared her throat. She caught my eye and giggled.

Gods, she was so happy. What the hell was I doing? I managed a nervous chuckle.

The couple and dog wandered by giving us suspicious glances, and her giggles devolved into laughter. Her mirth was contagious, and despite the panic, I found myself laughing along with her.

"I think that's our cue to leave," I said.

"Yeah, you're probably right." She yawned. "It's getting late." She placed a hand on my arm, and I stiffened, my feelings for her at war with my growing anxiety. "You're amazing, Elias." She squeezed. "Thank you for bringing me back to myself." She stood on her toes and kissed me on the cheek.

I stared down at her expectant face and swallowed, my mouth as dry as the sand. "You did that yourself, Lena. I just reminded you of your destination." I bent down and pecked her on the cheek. "Come on. I'll walk you home."

We walked up the beach toward the dunes, and the loud, steady beat of my pulse drummed in my ears, drowning out everything around me except for a single question: how had I let this happen?

My arms sliced through the waves like propellers through air, and my heart thumped hard against the walls of my chest as I pushed myself to my physical limits. My lungs burned with exertion, and I prayed to the gods it would mask my burning desire for Lena.

"Elias! Dude! Hold up!"

Niko's voice snapped me out of my self-inflicted punishment, and I stopped, nostrils flaring.

"What the hell, man?" Niko was panting even harder than I was. "Are you trying to kill us?"

"No. Sorry. I—" I dragged a hand down my face.

His forehead creased, eyebrows reaching for his hairline. "Man..." He shook his head, stupefied. "She's got you all twisted up, doesn't she?"

My jaw clenched. "Shit, Niko. I can't get her out of my head."

"Why? Cause she didn't fall all over you like everyone else? Is that what this is about?"

"No." I shoved a hand into my hair and tugged. "I mean, it was, at the beginning, but—it's more than that."

Images of her face flashed through my mind. Our swim with the dolphins when I'd first seen her smile. Her surprise and delight the day I'd shown up for her yoga class. Her parted lips and lidded eyes when I'd made her come.

This went far beyond a challenge, and it freaked me the fuck out.

"Don't tell me Elias Georgiou has *feelings* for a woman." Niko grasped his throat as if he was choking, rolled his eyes back, and sank under the water. When he emerged, he sputtered as he laughed.

I looked out at the horizon and ground my teeth. I didn't need his shit. I was beating myself up enough as it was. I didn't want to hurt her, but...

I snapped my attention back to Niko, determined. "Open mic tonight?"

He arched an accusatory eyebrow. "You sure about that?"

"Abso-fucking-lutely."

And before he could unleash any more commentary, I dove into the water.

CHAPTER ELEVEN
LENA

At the southernmost tip of Hilton Head, South Beach hosted the largest open mic on the island. The tourist-trap of the Salty Dog Café always drew a crowd, and tonight was no different. Elias hadn't mentioned it during our date two nights ago, but it was well attended, so I had no doubt he'd be there.

I liked him. And after the past few weeks, I trusted him, which should have scared the hell out of me. But I'd gotten to know him, and found him genuine, empathetic, and sincere.

And sexy, Lena. Don't forget unlawfully sexy.

Memories of his voice alone began a trembling ache deep inside me. And the way the moonlight highlighted his sun-streaked hair as I ran my fingers through its silky waves. How he'd kissed me, gently at first, but then raw and hungry. How he'd ripped off my thong... I shivered at the memory.

I had a weakness for athletic bodies, but my attraction to Elias went far beyond lust. His passion for life, his energy and positivity, the ease and carefree abandon with which he walked through his days, had dredged my sunken spirit up from the depths. His bright energy shined like the sun over everyone around him, and I wanted to soak up more of his vitality.

I walked past the swimming pool, across the parking lot, and into a wall of people packed into the shopping and dining complex surrounding the marina. There was a tennis tournament in town, and the restaurants, shops, and bar of the most popular spot on the island bustled with nightlife.

I couldn't wait to see him. We'd texted a couple of times since our date, but with all the tourists in town, he'd been busy with work, so this would be a nice surprise.

I weaved my way through the throng and wedged myself into a sliver of space at the bar. I ordered a drink and leaned against the sticky surface to people watch.

A sound tech adjusted the mic atop the stage. Long lines of couples and families extended from the entrances of both restaurants. Impatient kids vibrating with excitement awaited their turn with a clown making balloon animals. And my ex-husband...

Oh no.

Oh no, no, no, no, no, no, no.

What the hell is he doing here?

I hid my face with my drink and watched him. He strolled through the crowd with irritating overconfidence and turned his head down and to the side to a young woman in a tennis skirt swinging her hand in his. A young woman half his age. A young woman who was *not* the young woman he'd left me for. What an asshole.

He glanced at the bar, and our eyes locked.

Damnit!

My head snapped to the bar to break eye contact, but it was too late. He'd seen me. And in the heartbeat our eyes met, he'd scowled, only to plaster the fake smile I'd lived with for nearly a decade across his face a moment later. He bent down to his "friend," whispered in her ear, and lifted his chin in my direction. She glanced at me and nodded, then stalked off in a huff, flipping her hair as she went.

I rolled my eyes and slugged down the rest of my drink.

He stopped in front of me, hands shoved into his shorts, and rocked up onto the balls of his feet and back down again. "Lena," he said.

"Rob."

"I heard about your grandma. Is that why you're here?"

I held up the dregs of my drink and plastered "duh" across my face.

He nodded. "Sorry to hear she passed. She always liked me."

Typical. Always about him. "Until she didn't."

He shrugged, and the gesture did not have the same endearing quality it had when Elias did it.

"What are you doing here, Rob?"

"Heidi—" He hitched a thumb over his shoulder. "—is in the tennis tournament. She invited me down. Decided to make it a vacation."

"Ah. Heidi, is it?" My voice turned thick with spite.

"Yeah. She's great."

I launched an eyebrow into orbit. "Until she isn't, right?"

He locked his lips together tight, no doubt working hard to cage a biting retort. An awkward silence hung in the air.

"I signed the papers."

"Did you want an award?"

He folded his arms across his chest and raised an eyebrow.

More silence.

"Well, I guess that's it then," he said.

"I guess so."

He stared at me, and I'd be damned if I broke eye contact first. With a final nod, he spun on his heel and walked away.

I let go of my breath, and my shoulders slumped. I waved at the bartender for another drink, and thankfully he delivered in record time. I picked up the brandy and diet with a shaking hand and sucked half of it down in one gulp, trying to wash away the bitterness and doubt resurrected by the chance encounter.

I'd trusted Rob once, believed the façade, and look

what happened. Was I doomed to repeat history? Was this thing with Elias just part of some sick pattern I'd learned to play on repeat?

There goes Lena again, setting herself up to be abandoned.

My stomach heaved, and I covered my mouth with the back of my hand.

"Good evening, Sea Pines. Welcome to South Beach."

A deep voice boomed through the night over the PA, driving my attention toward the stage and out of my downward spiral.

"Welcome, vacationers. Welcome, tennis fans. Welcome, locals!"

A couple of loud whoops sounded from behind me atop sporadic clapping.

"We want to get this night started out right. So, here to kick things off is a local favorite—Elias Georgiou."

The tourists politely clapped, but the locals whooped even louder. A group of enthusiastic women at a table near the front squealed and clapped their hands overhead.

A pang of jealousy reverberated through my chest. Seeing my ex had dampened my mood and made me question my faith in Elias. His personality didn't have the same undercurrent of fake as Rob, but I'd been fooled before, and now doubt invaded my trust.

He climbed the steps to the stage, acoustic guitar slung across his shoulder. He wore a black Grateful

Dead t-shirt that hugged his broad chest and thick biceps atop faded jeans that hung low on his narrow hips. He leaned into the mic. "Hey. I'm Elias." More whoops from the crowd. "Hope you're having a good night."

Damn, he was so charming and engaging, and he hadn't even started singing.

"Sit back, relax, and enjoy." He flashed his crooked Hollywood smile, and the ladies in the front squealed with delight.

A fresh wave of unease rippled through me. I rolled my shoulders, determined not to let my encounter with Rob ruin my night.

Elias's voice floated on the warm night air like an enchantment, dancing across the distance to entwine me in its magical embrace. The world fell away—the doubt, my ex, Elias's fan club—and only his song remained, caressing my soul until it wanted nothing more than to adore him.

His performance ended as quickly as it began, the sudden absence of his music creating a vacuum. I stood, the pull of his voice drawing me toward him for more. But I wasn't the only one he'd bewitched. The packed marina erupted with applause and cheers— another standing ovation—and I lost Elias when he stepped down from the stage and into the crowd.

I slapped a twenty on the bar and like a magnet drifted mindlessly toward its pole, the echo of his notes on my soul compelling me forward. I needed to hear his voice again and bask in its energy.

The crowd packed in tight trying to get closer to the stage. I squeezed through, creating a path for myself between eager fans until I could see him.

He stood with Niko, the women from the table pressed into a tight circle around them, doe-eyed and shoving hips and breasts into noticeable positions. One of the women grabbed his bicep and stood on her toes to whisper. He leaned down to meet her, offering his ear. After a moment, his eyes went wide, and he threw his head back in laughter. He wound his arm around her waist and pulled her close. She rested a palm on his chest, and he placed his hand over hers. Then he winked at her, and the spell of Elias's voice shattered with my heart.

I reeled from the visual slap in the face and averted my eyes. I looked past the crowd only to have my gaze land on my ex-husband grabbing his tennis girlfriend's ass.

The world spun, my past and present colliding in a dizzying hurricane of betrayal. I lost my balance and careened into the body next to me.

"Excuse me," I muttered to no one.

My attention gravitated back to where my biggest life mistake was playing out on repeat and found Niko staring at me, concern and disappointment evident in the wrinkle of his forehead and hard set of his jaw.

I blinked hard, spun away, and mindlessly pushed through the crowd into the parking lot. I stumbled to my car, moving my body parts like a robot set to automatic. Headlights streamed past me as I drove, blurred streaks through unshed tears.

I got out of my car, walked into the house, and fell into bed still fully clothed. I didn't care. I squeezed my eyes shut to block out the emptiness surrounding me and willed sleep to rescue me from my waking nightmare.

CHAPTER TWELVE
LENA

I blocked his number after the tenth missed call. I'd lost count of how many unread text messages I'd deleted, no doubt variations of the first.

> Lena. Please pick up. I'm so sorry.
> Give me a chance to explain.

There was nothing to explain. We weren't in a relationship. We hooked up once. He didn't owe me anything, and I didn't owe him a chance.

I didn't want or need that kind of drama in my life. Especially not now. Better to end this before it started for real and move on. I'd learned my lesson the hard way with Rob, and I wasn't about to ignore the signs and pretend like Elias was anything other than what he was—a smooth-talking playboy with wandering eyes and no sense of commitment.

Despite my mature, adult reasoning, my heart

ached with disappointment, a fresh pang of loss reminding me of how far I'd come over the past month and how far I would fall if I didn't cut this off.

I liked Elias. Really liked him. I had trusted him. I had thought his interest was genuine. Everything about our friendship and the feelings I'd developed rang true. What I'd witnessed the night before seemed like an anomaly, a big misunderstanding. But that was wishful thinking. That was romantic Lena talking, and I refused to let her explain away his behavior. I refused to fall into another trap.

I rode my beach cruiser to Harbour Town determined to resume my routine and ignore the painful splinter of disappointment wedged in my chest. It didn't matter. Elias's fuckery didn't change my plans.

I locked my bike to the rack in front of the breakfast café and waved at Sonia as I walked in, standing behind the counter and taking orders. A line had already formed, even this early in the morning, and I patiently waited my turn.

"The one with the dark hair. His voice and his muscles and those eyes..." A woman's bubbly voice carried over the din of the café.

I glanced over my shoulder at two young women sitting at a table near the door.

"No way. The blond. The way he looks at you when he sings..." The other woman's voice had a daydreamy quality, and I could imagine her staring off into space with doe eyes. She let out an over-exaggerated sigh. "I felt like one of those teenagers from the fifties ready to fling my panties at Elvis."

Her friend's shrill laughter pierced the peaceful sounds of the coffee shop. "Oh my god, Sadie! Yes! I wanted to throw myself at that dark-haired Greek god. Those two were unreal."

"Unreal is right. Do you think those old island legends are true? That there are sirens on Hilton Head? Maybe those two sexy singers are demons luring us in with their voices." The two women burst into a fit of giggles, and I rolled my eyes so hard I thought my retinas might detach.

Despite their cringey fangirling over the man who'd stomped on my heart, my brain caught on the island legend comment, the stories from my childhood reemerging into the forefront of my thoughts.

I'd dismissed the idea in the past as ridiculous, but this time my gut latched onto the possibility and wouldn't let go. Grandma had always said the island had magic, and she'd raised me with an appreciation for the supernatural. Until now, mythological creatures walked the line of being too out there, even with my spiritual upbringing. But now?

I stepped up to the counter. "Hi, Sonia."

"Good morning, hun. Triple latte and a raspberry scone?"

I'd been coming back to the café regularly since that first visit, relishing the routine and Sonia's company. "You got it."

I glanced over my shoulder to see if anyone else was waiting. Nope. Just customers enjoying their breakfasts.

"Remember those old stories Grandma used to tell about sirens on the island?"

She quirked a wry grin, and her eyes sparkled with amusement. "You know your grandma and I never saw eye-to-eye on that sort of thing. A lot of mystical mumbo-jumbo, if you ask me. But yes, I remember the stories."

"It's been so long. I have this vague recollection of creatures enchanting locals with their voices, but... I'm fuzzy on the details."

"You want the story."

I nodded.

"The sirens." She sighed and looked up as if accessing long-forgotten memories. "That rumor has been floating around for years. Even when I was a young girl. They say a group of sirens emigrated from Greece around the turn of the century to escape persecution. They searched the coast of America for a place to settle, somewhere reminiscent of their Mediterranean home, and—" She held her arms open. "—they landed here."

I raised a skeptical eyebrow, and she laughed. "I know, it all sounds a bit far-fetched, doesn't it? And the rumors started a *long* time ago, back when my mama was a child and when women weren't allowed to be as *casual* in their relationships. And the island *has* been home to a couple of legendary singers over the years, just feeding the rumors. Mama used to warn me off the island singers, telling me I'd be led astray." She chuckled and waved a dismissive hand. "Old-world superstition if you ask me, the lot of it."

"What about now?"

"Now? Well. I'm too old now to be out and about listening to gossip. But if there's any truth to the rumors—" She jutted her chin in the direction of the table by the door. "—I'd put my money on those Georgiou boys." Her face took on a mischievous bend. "Yes, I overheard the ladies talking, too. Your grandma and I knew their fathers, and those men were just as charming and notorious as their sons. And those voices!" She fanned herself with a menu. "No doubt there's something magical about the men in that family." She narrowed her eyes and scanned my face. "Why do you ask?"

I looked away. "No reason."

"Lena?"

"Ugh. Those swim lessons I've been taking?"

"Uh-huh."

"I've been taking them with one of the instructors from the Ocean Explorers Club and—"

"Ahh. I see." She chuckled again. "A little enchanted by Elias Georgiou, are we?" My cheeks heated. "You're not the first, and you won't be the last. He's a handsome one, all right." Her eyes landed over my shoulder, and I glanced back to see a new customer in line.

"Thanks for breakfast, Sonia. And the story. I'll see you tomorrow."

"Anytime, hun," she said with a nod, and I turned to leave.

I stepped out onto the porch and found an empty bench to enjoy my breakfast while the world went by —couples out for a morning stroll, the *thwack* of tennis balls from the court across the parking lot, golf carts carrying players to their next tee.

Elias said his grandfather and his great-uncle had emigrated from Greece. And Elias and Niko were in their mid-forties...

I took a bite of scone and washed down the sweetness with my latte.

I remembered how the words he sang to me that first night lodged in my head, playing on repeat as if they'd had a life of their own, their haunting tone and magnetic allure constantly demanding my attention...

I sipped my latte, hoping the milky comfort would temper the nervous seed forming deep in the pit of my stomach.

And while he sang? Sometimes even when he spoke? His voice drew me to him like a moth to a flame. It captivated me, compelling me toward him to beg for more. I'd experienced it on more than one occasion, but wrote it off as my lusty, sex-starved body winning the war with my brain. But maybe that wasn't the reason. Maybe the island was home to another, more corporeal form of magic.

The nervous seed took root, a combination of

unease and anger spreading out from my stomach into my chest and up my neck. A siren. A magical creature. Seducing me with his song and manipulating me into believing we had something special. Then moving on to his next victim.

"This just keeps getting better, doesn't it?"

I struggled to sleep that night, the endless reel of racing thoughts about Elias, sirens, and moving to Hilton Head speeding across my mind like an action movie trailer on repeat. I'm not sure how or when I finally succumbed to sleep, but I found myself transported into the kitchen amid the sights, sounds, and smells of a waking dream.

I stood behind Grandma at the standing mixer, her hand on the lever watching the batter come together. She was making my birthday cake. Coconut with fresh strawberries. I'd watched her do it every year as a child, and even after I moved out, she made it for me when I came home as close to my birthday as possible.

The smell of the coconut and sugar and the rhythmic whirr of the standing mixer penetrated my senses even through sleep. A bowl of sliced strawberries sat on the counter waiting to adorn the final product. I stood behind her, peering over her shoulder, and warmth radiated from her slight frame. Familiar. Comforting. Real.

She glanced back, the wrinkled features of her face

filled with love and pride. She tipped her head and touched her forehead to mine like she'd done ever since I was little. A sense of safety and belonging swelled in my chest, a reflection of her unconditional love.

"I'm so proud of you, Lena. Trust your instincts—you know the truth. And never give up." She held my gaze a moment longer as if to ensure her message landed, then turned back to face the mixer.

I woke with a start, and Grandma's sudden disappearance ripped the scab off my still-healing heart.

I cried. Hard and unrestrained, I cried. Not the bitter, frustrated crying I'd done after my divorce. Not the sad, defeated crying I'd done after Grandma died. But a complete and uncontrolled emptying of emotion.

Everything came out in big, ugly sobs that wracked my body and expelled every last drop of self-doubt, worry, and grief. And when there was nothing left, when the well of my emotions had been tapped dry, I let out a final, pained sigh.

Dazed and dizzy, I sat up and worked to catch my breath, my body aching from the emotional release. I grabbed a tissue, wiped my eyes, and blew my nose. I drained the glass of water on my nightstand and let out a long, shuddering breath.

A quiet peace descended upon me, a grounded calm after an emotional storm, and with it came clarity. I had a plan. Everything else was noise.

I glanced at my phone. Six o'clock. Perfect. I picked it up and made the call.

"Yoga Star Charleston. This is Candace. How can I help you?"

"Hey, Candy. It's Lena."

"Hey, girl. It's early. Everything okay?"

"Everything's fine. I just wanted to see how things were going and run something by you. Do you have a minute?"

"The six a.m. just started so, yeah, I have the next hour and a half free."

"Great." Might as well get right to it. "How would you feel about managing Yoga Star Charleston?"

"I already manage Yoga Star Charleston."

"No. I mean, by yourself." I paused. "Like, without me there."

Silence.

"Uh… Lena? What are you talking about?"

"I want to expand the business. I want to open Yoga Star Hilton Head." My body buzzed with anticipation.

A loud *thunk* traveled across the line followed by a high-pitched squeal. I held the phone away from my ear until the piercing noise stopped.

"Candy?"

"Sorry! Sorry, I dropped my phone, because I am So! Freaking! Excited!"

She squealed again, and I held the phone away, laughing at her enthusiasm. "Yeah?"

"Are you kidding?"

"It's going to be a lot of work, especially while I'm busy getting the new studio ready—I'll be refurbishing an existing space."

After resolving to stay on the island and expand my business, I'd spoken with Harry about buying Hot Yoga Hilton Head. I had a nest egg from selling the house in Charleston, enough to cover a downpayment and repairs, and knew I could breathe new life and a fresh energy into the space. When I'd offered to buy the studio, his eyes flooded with tears, and he lifted me off the ground in a giant bear hug. The entire arrangement seemed fated and brought with it a renewed sense of purpose. Nothing could deter me from this plan, not even my revelations about Elias.

"I know I can handle the extra responsibility," she said. "I want to handle it."

"I have no doubt, Candy. I trust you. You're... family."

"Aww! Don't make me cry!"

I let out a nervous chuckle, my own eyes welling with tears.

"This is a good move for you, Lena. You need this." The sincerity in Candy's voice threatened to push me over the edge. "You've sounded so much happier over the past couple weeks. Happier than you've been in months. You needed the change of scenery, especially after the asshole." A beat passed, caught on her last word. "Sorry. It's just... he really is an asshole." I laughed, and the tears spilled over. "Anyway, this is an opportunity for a fresh start. A new beginning for both of us!" More squealing. "I'm so excited!"

What a relief. I swiped at the happy tears trailing down my cheeks. "Me too."

And that was the truth. I really was excited. Excited to walk out of the past and into the future. Excited to build a new community—a new family—here on the island. Excited to call this place home.

CHAPTER THIRTEEN
LENA

That night, I stood at the water's edge. The crescent moon cast a soft glow across the water, and a warm wind carried the humid air through my hair. I wrapped my arms around myself and allowed the slow, rhythmic crashing of waves to lull me into meditation.

I had connection and community in Candace. I had love and support in Sonia and the memories of my grandma. And I had a fresh start and future in my plan to expand Yoga Star and stay on the island.

While pangs of sadness still hit me from time to time, the deep depression that had weighed on me for so long had lifted. Life felt light and full of possibility. And I'd be lying to myself if I didn't acknowledge the role Elias played in my recovery.

The truth? I'd let Elias into my heart. The easy friendship we'd developed over the past few weeks and our sizzling beach hookup had unlocked the vault.

He'd gotten me to trust again, no simple task after what my ex had put me through. And unlike Rob, Elias's personality and flirting weren't a manipulative act. He had a big heart and spread his positivity and optimism wherever he went, genuinely opening himself to others. I wanted to give him the benefit of the doubt, but I'd been scarred by my past, and I struggled to reconcile what I'd seen that night with my faith in his virtue. And now my trust also snagged on the island legends.

Was Elias really a siren? A mythical creature? And if he was, how much of what I felt was real? Was I under the influence of his song?

I wanted to believe he wouldn't manipulate me and use his power to affect my emotions. But then again, I didn't exactly have the best track record at gauging my partners' intent or integrity.

I shook my head. This whole train of thought was bananas. A siren? Was I really considering this as a viable possibility? No matter what, though, I couldn't deny the island's magic. I'd felt its mystic energy, my grandma's spirit, and the role they played in my transformation. Was it really such a huge leap to think magic extended to supernatural beings?

Notes floated along the warm ocean breeze from somewhere distant. I tried to ignore the sound, assuming it came from one of the resorts, but the song grew louder and the music edged closer. Words took shape, and the haunting melody drew my attention south and tugged on my body.

A man, backlit by the faint moonlight, waded through the shallow water toward me. His pant legs were rolled up, the waves lapping his muscled calves, and his longish hair moved with the breeze. I knew that body. I knew that voice. Elias.

The song swelled and became insistent. I needed to go to him. I fought the impulse, but then he faced me. His voice rose and reverberated through my body, capturing control, and holding me in place. His eyes glowed, luminous in the darkness, crystal blue pools of ocean reflecting the crescent moon.

My arms fell to my sides, and I took long, slow strides toward the relentless pull of his voice. I moved without thought closer to the enchanting man with gorgeous eyes and a sad downturn to his mouth. My brain caught on his lips, shaped into a frown, so unlike the carefree smile of the man who'd captured my heart.

He reached for me, and I took his hand. He pulled me into him, wrapping an arm around my waist and holding my hand as if we were dancing. His voice softened, and he sang the final, quiet words into my ear. His breath caressed my neck, and the rough edge of his stubble brushed my cheek. I melted into his arms.

He held me closer, sensing my surrender, and nuzzled my neck. In a daze, the vestiges of his song echoing through my mind, I inclined my head to give him better access, and he rewarded me by trailing feather-light kisses up my neck to my ear. He placed my arm on his shoulder and wrapped his hand around the nape of my neck, threading his fingers into my hair. He tilted my head back and stared at me with glowing blue eyes. My lips parted in invitation, and his eyes lidded as he bent forward to kiss me.

My pliant and willing body, spellbound by the music, his eyes, and his closeness, succumbed. His lips on mine were a welcome reunion; they'd gone missing and had found their way home. The tender stroke of his fingers through my hair and across my neck sent shivers down my spine. He massaged my mouth gently, his tongue sliding over mine in slow, careful caresses, and I surrendered to the delicious taste of his kiss.

He broke the kiss and squeezed me close as though he couldn't bear to have even an inch separating our bodies. "I'm so sorry, Lena." His enchanting voice was no more than a whisper.

Sorry? Sorry for what?

My mind swam in a sea of his song. I wanted to listen to his voice forever.

That thought scratched something at the back of my mind, but what?

It didn't matter. What mattered was that he'd stopped kissing me. I leaned forward and pressed a kiss against the top of his chest, tangling my fingers in his wavy hair.

"I didn't know you were there," he said.

Where?

I placed another kiss on his chest.

An incessant idea buzzed around my head like a gnat. I was forgetting something.

He kissed my neck just below my ear. Electric heat danced along my spine, from my neck to my core, and my knees weakened from the sensation.

"It's not what it looked like. Nothing happened. I made a mistake. I tried to tell you. I texted you, called you, but you wouldn't answer."

His soothing, sultry voice was oil on the flame of my desire. I stood on my toes to place a kiss on the edge of his stubbled jaw. He took my face in his hands and stared into my soul with those bewildering eyes.

"I knew if I kept coming here, I'd eventually find you. Get a chance to explain."

Had his eyes always glowed like that?

"I got scared. I thought if I admitted what was happening between us, I'd lose my freedom, lose my independence. But none of that matters if you're not in my life. I don't want to lose you.

"I fucked up, Lena. I'm sorry."

I fucked up, Lena. I'm sorry.

Those words. I'd heard them before. From my ex-husband. Standing in my kitchen next to a woman in her underwear.

I froze.

Images from the night at South Beach shot into my mind like a cannonball. My ex-husband. Elias singing. His arm around a woman as they whispered into each other's ears and laughed. The look on Niko's face when he saw me. The women at the coffee shop. The tales of sirens.

A surge of adrenaline ripped through my body and collected in my stomach. I felt dizzy and nauseated from the rush, but the flood lifted my brain fog and replaced it with cold clarity.

Confusion morphed into outrage, and I jerked out of his arms, my face contorting in horror. "Did you just sing to me?"

His mouth fell open. "Wha—What?"

"Did. You. Just. *Sing*. To. Me."

His eyes widened and darted across my face. "Yes. I —" His throat bobbed through a labored swallow. "You know I love to sing."

I narrowed my eyes, anger rising. "That's not what I mean, and I think you know it. You tried to manipulate me, didn't you? *Didn't you?*"

He stared at me in shock and shoved a hand into his hair. "I just wanted a chance to talk. To explain."

"So, you used your voice—your—your *powers*—to trap me? To make me listen?"

His face paled in distress. "Lena. It's not like that. I—"

"I think it's *exactly* like that!" Tears brimmed my eyes, frustration, anger, and hurt swirling in my chest even as the last vestiges of his song pulled me toward him. But I fought it. I fought it with every ounce of anger coursing through my blood.

My nails cut into my palms, fists balled tight from the effort of my restraint. I ground my teeth trying to contain the heated words begging for escape, but the look on his face—his sad eyes and worried mouth, as if *I* was hurting *him*—tipped me over the edge.

"How dare you!" I pushed him away with both hands. He barely budged, adding to my frustration. Hot tears streamed down my face. "How could you!" My fists landed on his chest, pounding against the immovable wall until I turned my back to him so he couldn't see me cry.

My shoulders shook trying to contain the anger and hurt. I wanted to storm off, but my legs wobbled with outrage.

"Lena. Please. Let me explain."

A gentle hand landed on my shoulder. I shook it off and spun around to face him. "No! You don't get to explain. You fucked up and tried to fix it by entrancing me. You tried to manipulate me!" I held up a staying hand, closed my eyes, and took deep breaths to rein in the anger.

"Lena—"

I opened my eyes, and my hand fell to my side. "I believed in you. I thought you were different." I shook my head. "But you just made this so much worse."

Before he could respond, I walked away, and under a riot of hurt and anger, my determined walk turned into a run. I didn't stop until I reached my house. Away from betrayal. Away from the siren. Away from Elias.

CHAPTER FOURTEEN
ELIAS

I fell to my knees, the pain in my head overwhelming the pain in my heart when Lena ran. I pressed my palms against my temples, and a strangled noise escaped my chest as the headache pierced my skull, the pain of my failed song punishing. And it would only get worse.

The compulsion to run after her and sing again, to ensnare her and never let her go, had me crawling on my hands and knees toward the dunes.

Tears formed in my eyes from the searing pain. Nausea rippled through my body in waves. I forced myself to fall to my side, holding my head until the worst of the initial shock dissipated. My stomach emptied itself onto the sand, over and over, each retch sending a white-hot spear into my already splitting skull.

Minutes morphed into hours, my body shaking

and heaving through the worst of the rejection, holding on for reprieve.

Finally, the backlash ended, leaving behind a dull throb and vertigo that kept the world spinning. The pain would return, each subsequent surge worse than the last until my song was answered or my body gave out.

I rolled onto my back and blinked open my swollen eyes. I wiped the crusted remnants of my stomach from my mouth with the back of my sleeve. A thin sliver of light peeked over the horizon. Dawn.

What had I been thinking? I hadn't been thinking; I'd been desperate. When Niko told me she'd seen me at South Beach flirting with another woman, I panicked. I ran to the parking lot, but she'd already left.

Texts, calls—I'd tried everything, even knocking on her door, but she wouldn't respond. The idea that I'd hurt her, that I'd lost my chance with her and relegated myself to a life without her, terrified me.

Niko was right; I'd been such an idiot. I thought I'd been protecting my freedom, but I'd been living in a prison of my own making. I'd convinced myself that the steady flow of adoration—one audience to the next, one woman to the next—meant I was set for life. There'd never be a shortage of devotion, however empty. Better than the alternative of opening my heart and tying myself to someone only to have them lose interest or be horrified by my true nature. For all the bullshit I talked about adventure, I'd never been willing to take the risk.

And what good was freedom if I couldn't share it with Lena? Without her, I'd never find freedom from the what-ifs and regret. I'd refused to look past my selfish need for independence and consider the possibility that life with Lena might be its own adventure, and instead of holding me back, she'd swim along with me.

The realizations were more than my rational mind could handle, and I became frantic to reach her. My siren's compulsion held an answer, and I'd eagerly—and thoughtlessly—followed its instinct.

I sat up, and the world spun around me. I swallowed back what would have been a dry heave and struggled to my hands and knees. I had to make it back to the house before the next surge of backlash attacked my already weakened body. With the little strength I had left, I hoisted myself to standing and stumbled forward, each step twisting a hot knife behind my eyes, the pain nothing more than I deserved.

CHAPTER FIFTEEN
LENA

I wiped down my mat, mopping up the sweat pooled there from practice. It had been especially hot, the heat and humidity amping up this late in May and adding their own punishment to the practice room. Only two other students had attended class, and they'd already left, so I tidied up the space in peace.

I rolled up my mat, walked into the foyer, and considered the studio, soon to be *my* studio. Harry had given me my own set of keys so I could come and go as I pleased while we finalized the sale. It would take at least a month to complete the transfer, and in the meantime, I could make plans for the refurbishment and help with teaching.

I gathered my things and walked outside, fishing in my purse for the keys to lock the door.

"Lena?"

I spun around to find Niko standing behind me,

hands shoved into his pockets and a hopeful yet worried bend to his tight mouth.

I had exactly zero desire to talk to him, especially if he was on some ill-advised messenger errand for Elias.

I'd wanted my anger to kill any remaining thoughts of forgiveness, but my outrage had dissipated over the past two weeks, replaced by memories of the hurt in his eyes, the sincerity in his voice, and the gentleness in his touch. Yes, he'd violated my trust and, worse, tried to manipulate me, but he *had* sought me out to explain, and my brain latched onto his words: "But none of that matters if you're not in my life."

Now, I wanted to give him another chance. Maybe that made me a pushover, but part of me—a large part of me—didn't care. I had picked up and put down my phone so many times over the past two weeks I'd lost count. Fingers hovering above the screen, trying to think of the right words. But each time, I put the phone down, determined to protect my fragile heart. I'd had to carefully stitch it back together again, and it was barely holding in one piece.

"Niko. What are you doing here?"

"I—" He cleared his throat. "I stopped by your house, but you weren't there. I need to talk to you." His voice sounded tentative, his words clipped and halted with worry.

I frowned. "What's wrong?"

He ran a hand down his face, and his eyes darted

around the parking lot. "Can we talk somewhere private?"

Worry invaded my stomach. "Sure. We can talk in here."

I unlocked the studio, and we went inside. I flipped on the lights and gestured to one of the benches by the cubby holes, but he shook his head and started pacing across the foyer.

"What's going on, Niko?"

"It's Elias." He stopped pacing and squared his shoulders to face me. "He'd kill me if he knew I was here, but..." His jaw twitched. "He's my best friend. He's my family. I can't watch him do this to himself."

I narrowed my eyes in confusion. "How about you start from the beginning?"

He examined his feet, clearly struggling through some inner turmoil. "Right. Okay." He shifted his weight from one foot to the other, wiped the palms of his hands on his jeans, and looked up. "Elias told me you know about us. Or, at least, he thinks you do."

He stared at me, waiting for acknowledgement. I replied with a terse nod.

He blinked, his eyes expectant as if waiting for me to run or pass judgment. When I did neither, he let out a breath and nodded.

"Right. So, you know about our compulsion, our need to draw people to us with our voices. The adoration, the devotion, the positive emotions it evokes in others satisfies our compulsion. It's why our song is inescapable." He paused, eyes shifting.

"Yes, I know you're sirens. I know you manipulate people with your voices." The words came out harsh and accusatory.

He glared at me. "That's not true." I scoffed. "But that's not the point and not why I'm here." He took a step toward me. "Look, if someone manages to break free of our voice—if someone rejects the song and walks away—it causes—it's like an emotional backlash. The compulsion turns inward and starts physically attacking us, trying to force us to sing again and capture the missing attention. And it won't stop until it's satisfied."

Realization struck, worry thickening until it was so dense my stomach dropped. "And Elias... Elias is being attacked?"

He nodded and continued his nervous shifting from foot to foot. "He made me swear not to tell you. Said he never should have sung to you and that it was up to you if you wanted to see him again. He thinks he deserves what's happening to him. But Lena—" He closed the final distance between us, and tears welled in his eyes. "Elias does *not* deserve what's happening to him."

I swallowed, but through my empathy, indignation rose. My patience for this entire conversation snapped.

"Then why don't you go find one of his groupies? I'm sure there's a long line of women eager to listen to him sing and shower him with praise."

The muscles in Niko's jaw clenched, his nostrils

flaring as he breathed. He pressed his lips together so tightly they turned white. "He wouldn't do that." His words came out clipped and biting.

"Really? Because from what I saw at South Beach, that's exactly what he'd do."

He tilted his head up to the ceiling and sighed, hands fisted then flexed, and bounced on the balls of his feet. "I'm not even supposed to be here." He swiped a hand down his face again and met my eyes. "Look. He could've sung to you again, you know that, right? Forced you to submit? He didn't. He wouldn't. And he could've sung to someone else. Anyone else. Hell, I begged him to. He flat out refused. Elias has never been good with this shit. He might be able to feel others' emotions, but he's never been in touch with his own." Sincerity blazed in his blue eyes. "But I know this—he's crazy about you, Lena, and he's torturing himself, thinkin' it's what he deserves for hurting you."

He grabbed my hand, and shocked by his profession, I didn't pull away. "If you have any feelings for Elias at all, if you're willin' to give him another chance, please come see him. He needs you." He dropped my hand and took a step back. "But if you don't, and I've misread this entire situation, I won't bother you again. It's what Elias wants. But I had to at least try."

He swallowed hard, searching my eyes one last time, then brushed past me and walked out the door. I stood frozen, my hand still outstretched where he'd held it, and tried to process what Niko confessed.

Elias was crazy about me. He'd refused all other women. He was sick—torturing himself apparently—and needed me.

Doubt warred with hope, indignation with compassion.

I'd latched on to the belief that I was reliving my life's biggest mistake, that once again I was falling for the wrong man. But when I examined that idea, it didn't hold up to even the slightest scrutiny. Elias wasn't my ex. The friendship, the respect, the trust. His personality, his vitality, his energy. All genuine. And as for the compulsion? The compulsion hadn't drawn me out of my depression. It hadn't taught me to swim. It hadn't come to my yoga class. It hadn't shared those intimate moments we'd had together on the beach.

My feelings weren't for the siren's song. My feelings were for Elias.

I grabbed my purse, locked up the studio, and hopped on my beach cruiser. I needed to get to him. Fast. I'd started down a path into my new future, and I refused to let the man who'd helped me see that path destroy himself. Especially when I wanted nothing more than my future to be by his side.

CHAPTER SIXTEEN
LENA

Elias sat reclined in a beach chair looking out at the ocean. Dark circles shadowed his eyes, and the usual brightness of his tan skin was muted under a thin sheen of sweat. He had a blanket pulled up to cover his shoulders. It was seventy-five degrees outside.

My heart cracked open to see this vibrant man so in love with life reduced to such a sickly state.

"Oh, Elias." I couldn't keep the exasperation or the concern out of my voice.

He turned his head and stared at me, unbelieving, like I was a ghost. "Lena." His beautiful voice croaked through cracked lips. "I'm going to beat the crap out of Niko."

"You're not in any condition to beat the crap out of anyone. Although, you're doing a pretty good job on yourself." I kneeled in the sand next to him and pushed the sweat-soaked hair off his face. "You stupid, stupid man."

The corner of his mouth twitched in a sad echo of his luminous smile. "Stupid doesn't begin to cover it." A pained expression replaced the almost-smile, a drawn look filled with regret and loss. "I didn't realize what I had—how lucky I was to have a chance with you." He swallowed as if trying to contain a wave of nausea. I searched for his hand under the blanket and clutched his cold, sweaty fingers. "There's nothing for me without you."

Given his current state, I knew he believed that, however dramatic, and the crack in my heart widened. "How long have you been like this?"

His jaw tensed. "Since that night on the beach. Since I sang to you. But this is nothing I don't deserve. I shouldn't have done that, Lena." Conviction shone bright in his glassy eyes. "It was wrong. I don't deserve your forgiveness, but please understand, if I could do it over, I wouldn't have used my voice."

I sat back on my heels, pinched the bridge of my nose, and sighed. "Yes, you would have. You acted on instinct. You're a siren. And a siren who happens to be completely out of touch with his feelings. Not exactly a great combination."

The corner of his mouth lifted again, and his eyes searched mine. "You're not surprised? You're—you're not horrified?"

"No, I'm not horrified. You're lucky I happen to be an open-minded, spiritually enlightened yoga instructor who was raised by an herbalist." I winked, and the muscles in his face relaxed. "But surprised? Yeah, at first. Although, I'm not sure surprised covers it. Skeptical and curious, maybe, followed by shocked and royally pissed off. Then resigned. And now accepting. You're going to have to be patient with me on the understanding part, though."

"Patient with you? What do you mean?" He swallowed again, but hope danced in his eager eyes.

I raised my eyebrows at his reaction. "Why do you think I came here?"

The blanket moved—Elias's easy shrug. "I—I don't know." The words came out a croaked whisper.

"Elias, for someone who is so wise about so many aspects of life, you really are clueless when it comes to relationships." I couldn't prevent the sharp edge of my tone. "What were you thinking?"

He grunted. "I'm a forty-five-year-old bachelor, Lena," he said dryly. "I wasn't thinking. I was freaking out."

I snorted, my mouth forming into a reluctant smile as I shook my head. "Fair enough. But I trusted you, and I thought you trusted me. You should have talked to me instead of pulling that stunt."

"I thought I was losing you. You wouldn't talk to me. I was desperate."

"I just needed time." I thought back to my dream and my grandma's advice. "Time to trust myself. Time to trust my instincts. They were telling me not to give up on you." I shifted my weight and squeezed his hand under the blanket. "And now I've had that time. Sing to me, Elias."

"What?"

"Sing to me."

He swallowed, and his eyes glistened with tears of gratitude, maybe, or hope. Hope that I'd forgiven him. Hope that we had another chance.

"Are—are you sure?"

"I've never been so sure of anyone than I am of you right now. Sing to me."

He smiled, one of his genuine, wide smiles that lit up any space. And under the rising moon, his eyes brightened as the first notes escaped his lips.

Pleasures be waiting by the sea
With a smile for all the world to see

His voice wrapped around me like a lover's embrace, and I opened my heart to its call. His eyes glowed a clear, penetrating blue, his siren's power pouring out through the dulcet notes. I leaned closer, wrapping both my hands around his neck, and his voice grew stronger.

Diamond waves through sunglass days go by
So beautiful to be here and alive

On the last word of the phrase he'd sung to me that first night at Shelter Cove, the phrase that had started my journey out of depression, I couldn't control my emotions any longer. My feelings for Elias spilled out of the crack in my heart, and I took his face in my hands and kissed him. Desperately and with all the longing and hope that had built up since that first night, I kissed him. With understanding and forgiveness, I kissed him.

His arms emerged from under the blanket, and he pulled me onto his lap as if that single kiss had broken a spell and given him back a measure of strength. He wrapped his arms around me, and I tangled my fingers in his hair as he kissed me with a desperation that matched my own.

Slowly, he gained strength. His hand pressed firmly into my back, and he moved his other arm beneath my knees. He pulled back from the kiss, and in a single, fluid motion that would have been impossible only minutes before, he stood and lifted me into his arms. His skin had started to brighten back to its normal healthy glow, the bags under his eyes fading, and he looked at me with that same carefree smile he usually reserved for the ocean and life's unending pleasures.

I ran the back of my fingers against his stubbled jaw. "It worked," I said, my words breathless with awe. "You're better. Your singing worked."

"It wasn't my singing, Lena. It's you. I'm better because you're in my life."

My heart swelled with affection, and I wound my arms around his neck and rested my head on his shoulder.

He took long, hurried strides toward the house and kicked open the door. Niko stood in the kitchen in swim trunks holding a half-eaten sandwich, mouth hanging open. I laughed and shoved my face back into Elias's shoulder. He jostled me in his grip and bounded up the stairs to the second floor of the beach house.

"Put me down!" I squealed.

"No way. Now that I have you, I'm never letting go." He carried me into a room and slammed the door.

French doors opened onto a balcony overlooking the beach. The warm ocean breeze fluttered sheer curtains under the romantic glow of moonlight, and waves crashed their rhythmic beat.

He set me on my feet but kept an arm around my waist looming over me. He pushed his hand into my hair, tipped my head back, and ravished me with his mouth. His tongue danced with mine in perfect synergy as though they'd been waiting for this moment to connect. We *had* been waiting for this moment to connect.

He slid his hand up the back of my shirt, found my bra, and with a flick of his fingers, undid the clasp. He pulled away long enough to drag my shirt and bra over my head and toss them aside before taking my mouth again and thumbing my nipple.

I groaned under his frantic touch, the feel of his rough fingers on my breast setting the space between my legs aflame. I craved his naked skin against mine. I tugged at his shirt, eager to run my hands along the ridges of his firm body and press my breasts against his muscled chest. He pulled free and yanked his shirt overhead. I took the opportunity to discard my shoes and shorts, and so did he. Then he picked me up and tossed me onto his bed. I laughed as I bounced atop the crisp white linens, cool like satin under my heated skin.

He climbed atop me and pressed his hips into mine. He was rock hard beneath his boxers, and I arched my back to grind myself into his hardness. He grabbed my wrists and held me down, arms pinned on either side of my head. He kissed me ferociously, teeth clashing and biting. He rubbed himself against me, and I squirmed under the delicious friction.

He broke the kiss, and before I could catch my breath, he took one of my nipples into his mouth and dragged it through his teeth. I yelped at the combination of pain and pleasure and thrust my breast up for more. He chuckled wickedly and obliged, sucking it deeper into his mouth before biting down, harder this time, and I moaned.

I dragged my fingernails down the hard planes of his back until I found the firm globes of his ass. As he tortured my nipple, I dug my nails into his muscles, pressing him toward me. I rubbed myself against him, desperate for more contact, the sensation of his teeth on my nipple not enough to sate the hunger between my legs.

"Fuck yes, baby," he said, voice gravelly with need. He rose to his knees, pulled off my panties, and tossed them aside. I scrambled to my knees, overcome with lust, took him by his shoulders, and pushed him onto his back on the bed. He lay there, eyes hungry, the muscles of his jaw twitching with strain beneath the roguish quirk of his mouth.

The length of his athletic body and his tented boxers painted a delectable picture. I licked my lips; I wanted to taste him.

His eyes dilated with anticipation, knowing exactly what I wanted. "You want this cock, don't you, Lena?"

I smiled, devilish. That's how I felt—devilish, powerful, and fabulous.

"Take it. Take my cock. Fuck me with your mouth, baby."

My lust spiked at his dirty talk. I pulled off his boxers, and wet pleasure surged between my legs at the sight of him, hard and full, thick head glistened with pre-come. I straddled his muscular thigh, ran my wetness against his leg, and dragged my nails up his sack. He shivered, and his hands fisted the sheets. I wrapped my fingers around the base of his cock, bent over, and slowly licked the tip. His eyes rolled back, and he groaned. I closed my mouth over his head and sucked. His body jerked and chest rumbled with deep sounds of pleasure. I rubbed myself against his leg as I pulled him deeper into my mouth, my head moving up and down in time with the movement of my hips.

He threaded his hands into my hair and tugged hard, urging me further down his length. I met his demands, turned on by his desire, and he grew harder and thicker in my mouth. I hummed with satisfaction, and he shivered from the vibrations.

"I need to be inside you," he growled. "Now."

He pulled me off him, gripped my hips hard, fingers pinching flesh, and flipped me onto my back. He spread my legs wide with his knees, took himself in hand, and placed himself at my entrance. He coated the head of his cock with my wetness while he devoured my mouth and, without hesitation, drove himself into me.

I cried out from the exquisite pain and solid fullness; he was big, and it had been a long time. He took my chin firmly in his hand and kissed me savagely, as savagely as he moved inside me with deep, forceful thrusts.

I raked my nails down his back, relishing his roughness and wanting more. My knees went wider, and I wrapped my legs around him, tilting my hips until I felt the weight of his balls on my ass. His unrelenting rhythm and the way he moved his body against my clit was too much. I reached the precipice of climax, desperate to come with his entire body pressed against mine.

"Elias! Yes!"

"That's it, baby. Come for me."

The power in his voice demanded, and I obeyed. I shattered into a quivering mass of sensation. With each stroke, the pulses of my orgasm thundered through my body, my moans accompanying them, deep and husky.

I gripped him tight until the shockwaves subsided and he slowed, my over-sensitive flesh twitching with each additional stroke. The tremors calmed, and he quirked his playboy smile as I brushed the sweaty strands of hair from my face.

"My turn," he said with a mischievous grin and pulled out.

He flipped me onto my stomach and pulled my hips into the air. I scrambled to get my hands under me and looked over my shoulder. Elias's tan muscled body glistened with sweat. He took himself in hand and the ache between my legs returned.

He met my eyes. "Do you want me to fuck you, Lena?"

My entire body shivered with need. "Yes," I said, my voice low and breathy.

"Tell me, Lena. Tell me what you want."

"I want you to fuck me, Elias. *Please.*"

He groaned and thrust into me. I cried out from the fullness at that angle. Damn, he felt good, and his deep strokes threatened to bring me to climax once again.

His pace increased, and I knew he was getting close. "Fuck, Lena!" He wrapped his hand around my front, dragging his fingers through our combined wetness and rubbed my clit ruthlessly. "I'm gonna come, baby. Come with me."

My orgasm came on slow but steady and strong. I screamed his name as it built momentum, and that pushed him over the edge. He grunted, thrusting hard, and his orgasm claimed him. He stilled, one hand digging into my hip, the other slowly circling my clit as he emptied himself into me.

He collapsed onto my back, wrapped both arms around my middle, and pulled me down onto the bed. He was still inside me, spooning me, leg draped over mine, our heavy breathing and the crashing waves loud in the otherwise quiet space. I took the arm wrapped around my waist and pulled it between my breasts, hugging him close, and kissed his fingertips. He snuggled in, nuzzling my neck, and kissed my shoulder.

"We should have done this weeks ago," I mumbled.

His chest rumbled with laughter. He brushed my hair aside and placed a soft kiss on my neck. "As much as I enjoyed that, it wouldn't have been right before, for either of us. We needed to get here in our own time."

He pulled out and nudged me onto my back. I wiggled around to face him, and his beautiful blue eyes were filled with adoration. He brushed his thumb across my cheek and gently kissed my forehead, then the tip of my nose, then each corner of my mouth.

"We needed to come to terms with our pasts so we could see a future. Our future."

Tears welled, my emotions threatening to overwhelm me—happiness, trust, pleasure, connection. My feelings for Elias ran deep, but they didn't scare me. Instead, they felt... right.

I pushed my fingers into his hair and ran my nails over his scalp. "Thank you."

"For what?"

"For giving me my life back. For showing me I can trust. For taking a chance with your future."

He leaned forward and kissed my lips, lingering there for a precious moment, then pulled back to meet my eyes. "*Our* future. And the adventure is just beginning."

EPILOGUE
LENA

SIX MONTHS LATER

"E!"

"Yeah?" Elias stuck his head through the half-open door and craned his neck until he found me. "What's up?"

"It's almost eight. Is everything ready out there?"

He stepped up and leaned easy, resting his forearm on the door frame. His t-shirt crept up, and my eyes locked on the ridge of his abs. I opened my mouth to say something, but nothing came out.

"Lena."

I tore my eyes away from my boyfriend's sexy midriff and found a wicked grin on his face. He winked, and I rolled my eyes.

"Sorry."

"You don't have to apologize to me, gorgeous."

He crossed the foyer and joined me behind the

counter. He slid his hands around my waist and rested his forehead against mine. Coconut and sandalwood assaulted my senses, and an ache of need rushed through me. I placed my hands on his chest, stared into his ocean eyes, and shoved down my desire.

"We could call off the whole thing, you know," he said with his siren's allure. He pressed his hips into mine, and I felt his hardness. "Lock the doors and do some... *partner yoga*." He waggled his eyebrows.

A bark of laughter escaped me, and I swatted him on the chest. "Stop it! I'm serious."

He ground his hips against me. "So am I."

"Elias!' I wiggled my way out of his arms, took his hands in mine, and stepped back. "Are we ready?"

He leaned forward and kissed my forehead. "We're ready."

"Good."

We'd been preparing for the grand opening of Yoga Star Hilton Head for weeks, and I wanted everything perfect for the big event. We had a small setup in the parking lot of the strip mall including a bar with beer and wine. Elias and Niko rented mics and hired a bongo drummer to accompany Elias's guitar. Island music for the win.

Candace and a few of my teachers from the Charleston studio drove down earlier in the week to double check the office organization and help prepare for the free classes we planned on offering to incentivize new clientele. But tonight, Candy was bartending, and my teachers would perform acrobatic partner yoga to demonstrate some of the new formats we'd bring to the island. Hopefully, the event would draw attention to the studio's rebranding and help establish my presence in the Hilton Head yoga community.

I patted his chest. "Everything in here is ready, too."

I stepped back and surveyed the inside of the empty studio—my studio—and nodded. Yeah, I was definitely ready.

"Hey." He grabbed my hips and pulled me back to him. "While we have a minute…"

I circled his waist with my arms. "What's up?"

"I have something for you." A pale blush of pink touched his tanned features. I'd never seen Elias blush before, and it made my heart ache with affection.

He shoved his hand into his pocket and pulled out a small, velvet box. My heart leapt into my throat, and my pulse pounded in my ears. I released his waist, and my hand shook as it rose to cover my open mouth. My other hand landed on my chest, covering my heart.

He stared down at the box, and his face heated to a brighter shade of red. Despite his siren's empathy, Elias had never been in tune with his own emotions, but right now, he was letting them lead, and I could tell how difficult it was for him.

"I'm so proud of you, Lena. What you've accomplished these last few months with the new studio. How you've handled everything life has thrown at you and come out stronger. You inspire me." His throat worked through a swallow, and he took a deep breath, held it, and then slowly let it out, his blue eyes glistening. "I love you, Lena."

Time stopped. Blood rushed to my face and tears welled.

His mouth opened and closed, his eyes searching mine for validation.

My Elias. My confident charismatic man so vulnerable and filled with hope. An evil grin took over my face—I couldn't help myself. "Took you long enough," I said playfully.

He let go of the tremendous breath, and his shoulders descended back down to earth, shuddering through a nervous chuckle. "I'm sorry. I should have said it sooner. It's just, I honestly didn't know what it was." He swallowed again, his lip quavering with the toll of baring himself so openly. "I've never been in love before."

"Oh, Elias." I threw my arms around his neck. He wrapped his around my waist and nuzzled his face into my neck. "I love you, too."

And I did love him. I'd loved him since our first night together at the beach house. I knew he loved me too but didn't have the words. Not until now.

He'd asked me to live with him three months ago, and I didn't hesitate to agree. My new life on the island had started, and it was hectic. Busy with renovations and preparations for the new studio, I wanted to spend as much of my free time with him as I could. But giving up my grandma's house wasn't an option. So,

Elias moved in with me, and Niko kept the beach house bachelor-pad.

My grandma's spirit was an ever-present and steadying force in my life, alive and well in my memories, in our house, and in the warm ocean breeze, comforting, supporting, and encouraging me every step of the way.

Elias pulled back and, with shaking fingers, opened the velvet box to reveal a single pearl set in a circle of aquamarine stones atop a silver ring. He was gifting me the ocean, and I gasped at its simple beauty.

"We both started to transform that first day we met on the beach." He lowered his eyes, blushing again. "Just like a pearl grows out of sand. And—" He cleared his throat and looked back up, eyes glistening with tears. "And I think now we're both fully formed."

He got down on one knee, and his hands shook as he took mine and held up the ring. Tears spilled down my face, and I let out a sob overflowing with happiness and love.

"Lena Sommer, you unlocked a hidden place in my heart that I can't wait to explore. Will you go on the adventure of a lifetime with me?"

"Yes! Oh, Elias, yes!"

He leapt to his feet and kissed me while I cried tears of joy, then slipped the little piece of ocean onto my finger.

The door slammed open, and both our heads snapped to attention. Candy stood frozen in the doorway and let out a high-pitched shriek that echoed through the studio.

"What's going on? What happened?" Niko stepped up behind her. "Holy shit!"

Elias and I devolved into nervous laughter, and Candy and Niko rushed us with hugs and congratulations. I looked around my studio and at my friends—at my family—and knew I was home.

THE END

Thank you for reading!

If you enjoyed this snack-sized read, check out The Art Collector, another standalone in my Demons Among Us series of contemporary paranormal romance novellas.

Or, if you're interested in a darker, full-length romance, try Her Dark Salvation, the first book in my paranormal mafia romance series Bonded in Blood.

For news and updates, join my newsletter at www.katelynbrehm.com

AUTHOR'S NOTE

They say write what you know, and with this series, I took that advice to heart. Aspects of each novella pull inspirational threads from my life, and it would take another novella just to explain them all. Instead, I'll talk about two elements of *The Siren's Song*, sourced from my life, integral to Lena and Elias finding their HEA.

I took my first yoga class when I was eighteen. I quit classical ballet and dance after high school, and their absence left a noticeable vacuum in my life. I needed something to bring me back into my body, something to challenge my coordination and flexibility, something to marry movement with grace. By mere chance, I went to a yoga class at my parents' tennis club taught by a lovely Indian woman back before yoga hit the mainstream in any real way. It's been a long time since that first class, but I distinctly remember two moments—my first exposure to

Pranayama (breath control) and my first Virabhadrasana 1 (Warrior 1)—after which I realized, "This. This is for me." I dabbled on and off with my newfound fascination for a couple of years, but it wasn't until I moved to Cambridge for graduate school that my practice really took off. There, I discovered Baptiste Power Yoga, and my life changed forever.

Everything Lena describes throughout the book is drawn from my own experiences, the formal and informal training I've received over twenty years of practice, eight years as a group fitness instructor, and the massive impact yoga has on my life. Yoga helped me through some of my darkest hours, but also some of my brightest. It's been a constant, steadying force, an anchor to the present in the oft tumultuous storm that is life's journey. I wouldn't be where I am today without yoga, and I hope a window into its transformative power comes across in Lena's story.

Hilton Head Island is a truly magical place. My family has vacationed there since I was a kid, and I have so many fond memories—endless hours at the beach, shopping in Coligny Square, biking past alligator ponds, watching professional golfers on the greens, breakfast in Harbour Town. We'd gather as an extended family each night at one of the popular spots and listen to the folk singers cover "American Pie" while eating ice cream and getting our faces painted. I'll always cherish my time with my family on the island; it left an indelible mark.

There was even a real dolphin encounter, albeit far

less sexy and far more embarrassing. I was maybe eleven or twelve, and my cousin Sara and I went swimming a little farther out than we normally went, the water up to our necks. Sara floated on a boogie board, and I treaded water next to her facing the horizon. A dorsal fin arced out of the water only a foot behind where we swam. I ditched the boogie board—and my cousin—screaming, "Shark! Shark!" and swam for the shore. Poor Sara, abandoned to her fate, scrambled after me, and we both stood on the beach flailing our arms. A pair of locals set us straight, all the while shaking their heads and laughing at us out-of-towners. Needless to say, we both survived, even if our preteen egos didn't.

Thanks to everyone who contributed to this novella. It really does take a village, and once again, I'm indebted to your support and guidance. Skyla Dawn Cameron, Kel Crafton, Margaret Curelas, Rhonda Parrish, Nico Rosso, and Jen Udden—you made this novella possible. Thank you.

About the Author

Katelyn Brehm is a second-generation German-American and native of Milwaukee, Wisconsin. She grew up watching far too much Star Trek, so much so, she decided to dedicate her education and career to space exploration. When she's not reading and writing fantasy and romance, Kat works as an aerospace engineer at NASA's Jet Propulsion Laboratory. She lives in Pasadena, California with her husband and two cats, Mini Wheat and Pepper.

Visit Kat
www.katelynbrehm.com

ALSO BY KATELYN BREHM

Demons Among Us

The Art Collector

The Siren's Song

Bonded in Blood

Her Dark Salvation

His Dark Vendetta (Coming 2025)